DISCARD

TRUCONFESSIONS

janet**tashjian**

SQUARE
FISH

Henry Holt and Company

For Doug, Warren, and Jake

SQUARE
FISH

An Imprint of Holtzbrinck Publishers

Library of Congress Cataloging-in-Publication Data
Tashjian, Janet.
Tru confessions / Janet Tashjian.
p.   cm.
Summary: Computer-literate, twelve-year-old Tru keeps an electronic diary where she documents her desire to cure her handicapped twin brother and her plan to create a television show.
[1. Diaries—Fiction.   2. Physically handicapped—Fiction.
3. Mentally handicapped—Fiction.   4. Twins—Fiction.
5. Brothers and sisters—Fiction.   6. Computers—Fiction.]
I. Title.
PZ7.T211135Tr   1997   [Fic]—dc21   97-16098

ISBN-13: 978-0-312-37273-6 / ISBN-10: 0-312-37273-6

Originally published in the United States by Henry Holt and Company
Designed by Meredith Baldwin
First Square Fish Edition: October 2007
10 9 8 7 6 5 4 3 2 1
www.squarefishbooks.com

Tru Confessions

DISCARD

KEEP OUT!

This is my private journal. My mother gave me the software package to use for homework assignments, but I can't stop playing with the journal feature. My best friend, Denise, uses the old-fashioned kind of diary with a tiny lock and key, but I need more space than that. On the keyboard, my fingers fly—I can write about my life, or gossip about my classmates, or even ⌨︎☞✆♌︎⚹✦✦◻︎ ▱⸸◯●▢▤◆⌨︎◹◆♑︎♒︎◆♅⌨︎☞✆⚭◻︎◼︎ ❖✦♎︎⸸◻︎ if I want to. Sometimes I just babble—stream of consciousness, Ms. Hinchey calls it—and sometimes I try to re-create a scene exactly as it happened: scenery, dialogue, and all. I guess I've never been able to make much sense of what happens until I write—or type—it all down.

But just because you popped up on my screen

like some computer virus doesn't mean I'm inviting you to stay and poke around my life. On the
other hand, I've got nothing to hide, at least no
more than any other twelve-year-old. You've heard
of that computer term WYSIWYG? What You See
Is What You Get? Same applies here. Don't say I
didn't warn you. . . .

ENTER AT YOUR OWN RISK.

Enough About You, Let's Talk About Me

Most of my friends call me Trudy, but Denise and my family call me Tru. I keep asking my mother if I can change my name to Leah or Jamie or some normal name. She won't let me because everyone in her family for two hundred years has been named after a famous writer. I tell her Judy Blume and Ann Martin are famous writers and they have normal names, but she says Gertrude Stein was a writer from the twenties and I should be proud to be named after her. My mother was named after Virginia Woolf—another great writer but a suicide case like my uncle Tommy.

Miggs Macrides heard Denise call me Tru, so now he calls me Falsie. He's one of those kids who thinks his jokes are still funny three days after he says them. I think jokes are like soda; they lose their fizz pretty quickly.

The reason I know so much about jokes is because I've been the butt of a few of them. Mostly by association. My brother, Eddie, has special needs and, unfortunately, that sometimes brings out the comedian in people who don't know him. I try to ignore the comments and have the relaxed attitude about life my mother has, but most of the time I end up worrying about stupid things—like homework, whether Billy Meier likes me, or if there's any disability in me. I worry about that last one because I'm Eddie's twin.

Asphyxia, that's what my mom called it—not getting enough oxygen. Poor Eddie was inside her suffocating and no one knew. I remember the day she explained it to me, I was bringing my bike into the garage. I asked her how to spell it twice, then traced the letters—a-s-p-h-y-x-i-a—on the seat of my bike with my finger. She didn't need to say it could have been me, 'cause I was thinking that already.

Eddie looks like my mother with his greenish eyes and dark brown hair. I take after my father— or so everyone says—with my blond hair and big ears. My mother says my father was a good guy (sensitive and well-meaning), but he just wasn't prepared for children, let alone twins, and one with special needs at that. He tried for the first two years of our lives to make it work, but when he got the opportunity to work in the Peace Corps in Africa, he jumped at the chance. My mom says it was probably the best thing, but I think charity begins at home.

My mother is a freelance graphic designer. Sometimes her work is in fancy magazines with her name printed in tiny letters along the side of the page. She works at companies for weeks or months part-time when they need help, then moves on to another place. Sometimes she even works on weekends. Because her computer is always set up on the dining room table, Eddie and I have learned how to use it, too. Especially Eddie. It's as if the ⌖ is a race car, the way he moves and clicks it across the table. He loves to make all kinds of cool drawings on the computer. I write captions for them and hang them around the house. Whenever we get invited to a party (which isn't that often, now that I think about it), I pick out the present and Eddie designs the wrapping paper.

My mother says I should work on my self-esteem, so she tries to get me to do exercises to improve it. I tell her I feel okay in the self-esteem department and that I should be working on my math homework instead. But she usually insists, asking me to visualize myself on top of a mountain. I picture myself on top of Mount Everest (or at least how it looks at the travel agency in the mall), then I act strong and powerful for the rest of the afternoon so she thinks I'm making progress. I try to tell her Eddie is the one who needs assertiveness training, since he's the one who gets picked on more, but she says future women—she never says girls—need all the help they can get. Besides, she says, Eddie has a special angel with him all the time. Well, I wish his angel would visit *me* once in a while, especially if it's invisible, so it can go into Ms. Ramone's office and find the answers to Friday's math quiz.

But if I did have a wish—make that two—here's what they'd be: to have my own television show and for Eddie to be un-handicapped. My mother says goals are just dreams with deadlines and that anything is possible if you're willing to do the work to make it come true. As far as my two wishes go, I wouldn't want to put a deadline on either of them soon.

I've always wanted to be on TV—in front of or behind the camera. My favorite toy as a kid was this microphone that amplified your voice (like mine needs any amplification). Mom says I used to carry it everywhere with me, calling out prices in the grocery store, doing play-by-plays for neighborhood sporting events. Because she's not a hambone like me, my mom can never figure out why I perform in front of any video camera I see. My favorites are the hidden ones at the bank and my grandfather's apartment building. The person who monitors the video cameras at the Bank of Boston probably groans every time I walk in. I like to think I add some entertainment to his or her day.

It's not like I'm some weirdo who just wants to be seen; who cares if the audience *sees* you if you don't have anything to *say?* I'm more like a director in training—digging up stories, filming documentaries that I hope will change the world. That's how I'll cure Eddie, uncovering some amazing new therapy through my meticulous research. Win the Nobel Prize while helping out my brother. All in a day's work.

These are the kinds of things I think about while I'm lying on my bed staring at the ceiling. I write my two dreams down on the palms of each hand, a to-do list tattoo. I don't really want anything else this year. Except maybe to go out with Billy Meier.

101 Reasons (Not Dalmatians) Why I Am Keeping This Journal

1. So that when I am a brilliant filmmaker and have my own on-line Tru Fan Club, you can download this journal and see what life was like before I was famous.

2. So that I can relive all my painful experiences just one more time to torture myself.

3. So if secret agents break into the house and interrogate me, I can tell them everything I know and still have a record on my hard drive.

4. To have something that's totally mine.

5. (Reasons 5–101 are still being compiled . . .)

Reasons Why Sometimes I Think *I'm* the One with Special Needs, Not Eddie

1. The way I pretend to be laughing at something really funny every time I see Billy Meier outside the junior high. The way I turned our only conversation—"What time is the assembly?" "Nine."—into the fact that he knows I'm alive.

2. The way I let Denise borrow my earrings even though I have to ask her ten million times to return them.

3. The way I sneak onto the Internet on my mother's computer looking for a cure for Eddie.

4. The way I still have fun playing Monkey Man with Eddie even though he figured out a few years ago that it's me and not a real monkey.

5. The way I actually write down script ideas as if I'll get my own show.

Ideas for My Television Show

- A large studio audience filled with people my age—but only people who Denise or I want to meet.

- An applause sign that goes on and off every few minutes so the audience can wildly applaud how funny and smart I am.

- A segment in the show where I bring out my bags and bags of fan mail. Then I read some letters out loud so my fans know that I really do care about them.

- A special part of the show where Eddie guesses the names of songs and the audience thinks he is amazing.

- Famous surprise guests who pop out from behind the curtain and hug me like a long-lost friend. The studio audience goes crazy, but I'm totally cool.

My Pathetic Idea of Fun

Okay, here goes. *(Don't laugh.)* I take my mother's video camera from the top of her closet, next to the paint-splattered jeans she uses to garden. I grab the tape marked "Home Movies" from my desk and slip it into the camera. Eddie and I wear hats and laminated press passes (you know, the kind real reporters wear) that I made by wrapping our school pictures in Saran Wrap. I take out my small chalkboard and write, "Tru and Eddie, Take One." Then I ask Eddie to click it in front of the camera. I yell, "Action," then follow Eddie around the house—eating, watching TV, trying to juggle. A few weeks ago, I had Denise jump out from behind the couch to scare him just to get a little drama on film.

I have Mr. Taylor to thank for helping me get so good with a video camera. He's my science teacher, and he does all the audio-visual stuff at school for assemblies and movies. Last year, he taught a class after school called Introduction to Video. Only three of us signed up, so we each got a lot of attention. He showed us how to edit film using our own VCRs, and brought in some equipment from home to dub in music. Ever since then I've been hooked. *(Technical information will be described in detail later. I'm not in the mood right now.)*

On days I want to be really obnoxious, Eddie and I go to the industrial park a few blocks away and film people leaving work. Sometimes I'll conduct a poll, like asking people if they think the sixth-grade art class should paint a mural on the wall of the building. I have them talk into my toy microphone, even though it doesn't really work. On those days, Eddie is the cameraman. He's a little inconsistent, but if you don't mind editing out the mistakes, he's okay. Eddie has filmed more sneakers and shoes than anyone else in history. Maybe that's why they call it footage.

Lots of directors got their start filming commercials, so I practice that, too. I ask Eddie to hold up a can of soup or an ice-cream cone and pretend he's trying to sell it on TV. He usually ends up getting the ice cream all over himself, a melting snowman talking into the camera.

After a while Eddie gets bored and drifts off to something else. I lie on my bed, hold the camera in the air, and interview myself. Because the camera is so close, when I play the tape back, it looks like I'm at the bottom of a well, like that Baby Jessica I heard about who fell into a well in her backyard. I ask myself how I got to be such a famous director and what my next project will be. Sometimes when I look up, my mother is in the doorway, shaking her head. I try to film her, but she puts her hand in front of her face, like she's Madonna walking into a restaurant. Then she takes the camera away and tells me I can talk to her friend Stuart anytime I want to. "Very funny," I say. Stuart is a psychologist specializing in compulsive behavior. If I ever did talk to him, I'd make sure to get it on film.

Reasons Why I Think My *Mother* Is the One with Special Needs

1. The way she doesn't care how she is dressed and goes to the market wearing sandals and wool socks in the middle of winter and asks the manager when he's going to start carrying organic vegetables.

2. The way she won't take us to Disney World because she thinks it's crass and commercial, even though Eddie and I have asked her a thousand times.

3. The way she gets down on her hands and knees at the beach whenever Eddie finds a shell or rock he wants to show her, and then stays down there in the sand—one time for half an hour— while I keep pacing back and forth.

4. The way she packs chopsticks in our lunch boxes when we have leftovers and encloses

a note written in fake Chinese letters with a translation at the bottom—something corny like "Have a rice day."

Just for the Record

Some of the technical terms used to describe Eddie:

- Developmentally Delayed
- Having Special Needs
- Intellectually Challenged
- Mentally Handicapped

He's not Down's syndrome, he's not autistic, he's just . . . Eddie. These labels don't give you a true picture. They don't tell you that he uses a knife and fork, rides a bike and plays soccer almost as well as I do. (I admit it took him longer to *learn* all these things, but what difference does that make in the end, anyway?) Physically, he looks like any kid our age. Sort of. It's really after you talk to him for a few minutes that you realize he might not be talking about the same thing you are. But then again, he might be. Confusing, I know, but you get used to him quickly. Besides, you can't go by me—I've known him all my life.

Beginning, Middle, and End

Our teacher, Ms. Hinchey, is talking about literature. She says good stories should have a beginning, a middle, and an end. Miggs says, "Duhhh," like isn't that so obvious, but I don't think it is. Sometimes a story can go around a few times, then back again, like a roller coaster. Or sometimes they start in the middle and go out, like the spokes of a wheel. I picture my life story as a wave: sometimes cresting, sometimes hitting bottom, then starting back all over again. I like Ms. Hinchey because she tells us stuff about her personal life. Like the time her husband ran over her sandals with the lawnmower, or how she finished her Christmas shopping in October. Ms. Brennan, the history teacher, is nice, too, but I don't know anything about her— like whether she has kids or not. If she does, I wonder if she makes them sit at the kitchen table in alphabetical order the way she makes us in class. And don't get me started on Ms. Ramone.

Ms. Hinchey asks us if we have any ideas for a class trip. I jump up and down in my seat like I'm in kindergarten and ask if we can go to the television station for a tour. Some kids think it's a good idea, but when Leftover, the class chowhound, suggests a tour of Pizza Palace, everyone goes wild. I'm disappointed, but still, almost anything is better than sitting in class all day.

On the way to the cafeteria, I peek inside Eddie's classroom. He's in one of the other sixth-grade classes, down the hall from mine. We're in different classes because we're twins, not because of Eddie's disability. Our school has the special-needs kids in regular classrooms with a resource person to help them keep up. The school board calls it "inclusion." As far as I'm concerned, the more Eddie gets included, the better.

From the hall, I watch everyone in Eddie's classroom working on different things. Eddie sits at the computer, rocking back and forth in his seat. The screen is filled with five or six planets and a few shooting stars. Mrs. Bell comes over and kneels next to him, speaking gently. One of my favorite things to do is to watch Eddie when he doesn't know I'm there. Sure, it's spying, but I don't think he'd mind. It's kind of comforting to see him out in the world, without Mom, without me. I suppose I watch him for my benefit more than his. I still never like to leave him alone for too long. Maybe it's a twin thing.

Being a Twin

I don't get to do anything cool like those girls in *The Parent Trap*, who confuse their parents and friends by switching identities. Being a fraternal twin doesn't give you that kind of flexibility. And it's not like Eddie and I have any secret ESP where he's two miles away, calling for help, and I hear him and race to the rescue. On our computer encyclopedia, I look up all kinds of twins, like Corsicans, where you punch one twin in the arm and the other one yells, "Ouch!" I stare at the picture of the Siamese twins for a long time—two old men in suits, joined at the waist and hip. If Eddie and I were connected, I wouldn't want to be face-to-face. Watching him eat up close for the rest of my life would definitely make me sick. If I had to, I'd settle for being joined at the legs. Maybe we'd be even better at soccer. I type "Mythology" into the computer and check out the picture of the Centaur. That's kind of what Eddie and I would be—minus the horse part. Galloping down the soccer field into the sky.

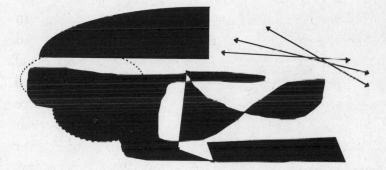

**Robin Hood at the goal line
—Eddie Walker**

(Computer drawing by Eddie; caption by me)

blah, blah, blah, blah,
blah, blah, blah,
blah, blah, blah, blah, blah, blah, blah,
I'm so bored.

Some Technical Mumbo Jumbo

- Editing—to take the film you've shot and put it in the order you want it. Usually, I use the equipment at school, but I can do it at home, too. I connect the video camera to the VCR with cables, then I play the tape while it's still in the camera and record it onto a blank tape in the VCR. The system at school is more sophisticated than mine, so the finished product is a little smoother when I do it there.

- Dubbing—to add in music, sound effects, or voices to the final tape (so it kind of sounds like it was filmed that way to begin with). I either have to go to the high school to use their equipment, or ask Mr. Taylor for help since my VCR isn't able to do this.

- Rewind—duh.

- Fast Forward—double duh.

(I'm a technical whiz, huh?)

Reasons Why Eddie Is the Best

1. He'll do anything.

2. He says things that seem to come out of nowhere that other people don't get but that I usually think are pretty funny. (Like when he calls the lady who works in the cafeteria Grampy. When Miggs heard him say that, he twirled his finger at his head like Eddie was crazy, but I knew he was calling her that because she has a thin gray mustache like our grandfather.)

3. He laughs at all my jokes (even the bad ones).

4. He'll give you anything you ask for in a trade and usually forget you didn't give him anything in return.

5. No matter how cranky and mean I get, he'll hang out with me anyway. (This counts as ten really great things.)

Reasons Why Eddie Is the Worst

1. The way he repeats the same thing over and over and over and over . . . "Hey, Tru. Want an apple? Do you? An apple, Tru? Here's an apple. Want it? Want an apple, Tru? Tru, want an apple?" AAAAAAARRRRRRGGGG-GHHHHH!

2. The way he needs to be reminded to brush his teeth and wash his face each and every day as if it's the first time he's doing it.

3. The way he can have real meltdowns sometimes, crying and screaming like a two-year-old having a temper tantrum. (Like when we couldn't get in to see *The Lion King* and he went ballistic in the lobby and Dawn and Laura from my class saw the whole thing and told everyone the next day. When Denise told them to get a life, they finally shut up.)

4. The way he burps out loud almost joyously in

the middle of the cafeteria even though I've told him a hundred times not to do it. (I have to admit, sometimes it *is* pretty funny.)

Surfing the Net for a Cure

I'm a pretty optimistic person usually, but today is a rainy Saturday and there's nothing on TV, and I'm trying to find some kind of help for Eddie. Drugs, an operation, even acupuncture—anything's a possibility. (As long as *I'm* not the one getting needles stuck in me.) My mother's at a meeting downtown and I'm surfing the Net on her computer. It only took me four tries to figure out her password, the same as her screen name. (Good security, Mom.) **Trued**—a combination of my name and Eddie's. Tried and true, that's my mom.

Three days ago, I left an e-mail message on the Net asking if anyone knew of a recent cure for someone like Eddie. I check the computer's 📭 and see that we have fourteen e-mail messages waiting to be read. Lucky for me, Mom uses the computer just for design and hardly ever checks for messages. I'll delete them all after I read them so there's no evidence that I've been tying up the phone lines.

The first e-mail is from **choppy** in Los Angeles. She—or he—says their son is developmentally delayed like Eddie and they've found great support in their school board. **Go4Ted** from Detroit says that his sister has special needs and is looking for a pen pal on the Net. **Misty77** asks what *my* problem is, that of course there's no cure for the mentally handicapped, and why don't I just ask the Lord for His assistance? None of the anonymous people who've answered my inquiry have anything helpful to say, except maybe for **deedee**, who tells me never to stop hoping and searching for answers. She/he sounds like Ms. Hall, who I had for social studies last year. It gets me wondering who **deedee** really is: A housewife in Iowa with curlers and long red fingernails? A businessman with a picture of his wife and two kids on his desk? A kid like me, trespassing into the adult lane of the information highway?

I log off before my mother gets home and go check on Eddie. He's got my mother's old record collection on the floor of his bedroom like some kind of vinyl carpet. Even though he can't read much at all, he knows the band and the name of the album just by looking at the label. I lean one of the albums against the wall (Dylan's *Blonde on Blonde*; Mom would kill me). Eddie and I take turns tossing M&M's at it until it falls. His shirt is untucked, his fingernails are dirty, but he's concentrating like a professional basketball player at the foul line. Just because there weren't any answers on the Net today doesn't mean there won't be tomorrow. We take turns pitching and eating M&M's until we hear Mom's car in the driveway. Then we quickly put away the records, turn on the TV and pretend we're watching something really great.

Eddie's Mind

No matter how off the wall, there is always a grain of truth to Eddie's stories. Today he told his friend Jerry that the church at the top of the street burned down—fire trucks, ambulance, two people dead, nothing left but the foundation. Jerry hopped on his bike and raced up the street, only to find the building still intact, in all its boring, glorious splendor. But Eddie wasn't making up the story to tease him. If you know Eddie well enough, you can always find a connection.

In this case, Eddie and I had gone to Denise's First Communion at that church. After the ceremony, an old woman had accidentally knocked a candle onto the floor. My mother picked up the candle and placed it back in the holder, making sure no sparks landed on the carpet. We never even talked about it. But in Eddie's mind, ⌀ + ✝ = THE CHURCH BURNED DOWN TO THE GROUND. Totally simple; I don't know why Jerry got so mad. But the *really* strange part of the story is that Denise made her First Communion four years ago. That's one of the great things about Eddie's mind. It doesn't matter if something happened ten years ago or the day before—yesterday, today, and tomorrow all blend into one (he probably wouldn't make a good historian). My mind works the opposite way—I worry about the past, present, and future before they happen, while they happen, and after they happen. And after all that, I *still* don't come up with anything half as exciting as a three-alarm fire.

Better way

Wish Number One

While I'm looking through the paper for my current-events class, and for my own journalistic curiosity, I spot an ad from the local cable company. (I watch the local station all the time. The Brazilian soccer and medical call-in shows are my favorites.) The ad says the cable company wants to be more involved in the community, so they are adding a second station and looking for additional programming, including a show created by and for teens. The headline of the article might as well say, "Trudy, We Want You."

It takes me a good five minutes to get the headphones away from Eddie to tell him. I hold my arms up like Vanna White on *Wheel of Fortune* and start singing "The Trudy Walker Show." Eddie joins in. One good thing about Eddie, he's always ready to join you, no matter what you're celebrating.

But, like everything in life, the fine print gets you every time. The station wants a full proposal— a list of three references, a show outline, an essay, and a fifteen-minute demo tape. All by the end of next month. My show idea suddenly seems as appealing as a bowl of soggy cornflakes.

When my mother comes home from grocery shopping, I show her the article. "It says the cable station will air the winning tape," I shout.

"Now we'll see how badly you really want this," Mom says. "In a city this size, I'm sure there'll be plenty of other applicants."

"Can't you just be excited?" I ask. What's her *problem?*

"I'm excited for you and for the other hundreds of kids who are reading that article right now and want their own television show." She balances a bunch of carrots in her hand as if they are on a scale.

What about visualizing myself on top of a mountain? What about doing the work to make my dreams come true? I take the carrots from her hand, stick them into the garbage disposal, and turn on the switch until pieces of orange carrot flesh fly around the sink. She shuts it off and when I pull the carrots out, the ends are gnawed and nubby.

Eddie comes in, takes the carrots, and pretends to eat them. "Ah, what's up, Doc?" He laughs and laughs, repeating the joke over and over—"Ah, what's up, Doc? Hey, Bugs. Hey, you pesky wabbit. Ah, what's up, Doc?"—but neither my mother nor I join in. I take the newspaper up to my room and start working on the proposal.

Before dinner, my mother comes upstairs. She tells me she lost a big job that afternoon because she wouldn't travel back and forth to New York City three times a week. She doesn't say it's because of Eddie and me, but I know it is. She plays with the beads of the friendship bracelet I am making for Denise. "About our conversation before, I guess I just wasn't in the mood for 'me, me, me,' " she says.

"I'll say."

"But that's no reason to destroy good food. You're too old for temper tantrums."

"Oh, but Eddie's not," I shoot back.

"Tru, cut me a little slack here, okay?" She strings two blue beads next to the black ones I already have on the bracelet. "Of course I think you should submit a proposal. Use the color printer for the final copy. It'll look more professional."

By the time she leaves, the design of the friendship bracelet has changed from an arrow to a kind of bridge. I decide to keep it and add on. But maybe she's right about the "me, me, me." Maybe the glitzy, glamorous *Trudy Walker Show* isn't the way to go. Maybe something more informational would have a better chance of being accepted. I start working on a new idea.

We are having fish for dinner with rice and no vegetable—probably some kind of punishment for the carrot incident. So before the plates are on the table, I draw some carrots on the computer with the art program and print out three color copies. I cut the paper carrots and put a few on each of our plates while my mother fixes the salad. First Eddie tries to eat them, then he gets the joke and just pretends. My mother looks mad when she first sees them, but then smiles and joins in, making loud smacking noises as if she enjoys these carrots immensely.

What People Would Say About Me If You Asked Them (Yeah, Right . . .)

She's the best friend there is: funny, smart, and loyal. She has a nice earring selection, too.

—*Denise Palumbo*

I would cut off my hand if she would go out with me, but she's too cool and I don't have a chance with her.

—*Billy Meier*

She revolutionized the way movies are made today. I'll be analyzing her next film for years.

—*Steven Spielberg*

She is the most loving daughter you could ask for. I'm so glad she's mine. It eats me up every day that I'm trapped here in Africa and can't be with her.

—*Mr. Walker*

I wish I didn't live in L.A., so I could see her. She is really cute, plus she seems like she'd be a blast to hang out with.

—*Brad Pitt*

One of these days I'm going to tell her how much I appreciate the way she helps me all the time: reading me books, wiping my nose, making sure I don't get lost. I'm really lucky to be her brother and especially her twin. *—Eddie Walker*

The entire school would come to a grinding halt without her. *—Mr. Manning, principal*

She is such a dream to baby-sit for. She never disobeys and is such a help with Eddie.

—Mrs. Hannah

She has a very active imagination; I wouldn't be surprised if she has a career in the arts. One thing I do know is that she's going to be a wonderful woman. I can just tell. *—Virginia Walker*

An Offer They Can't Refuse

I've been setting my alarm for six o'clock every morning so I can get up and work on the proposal for the cable station. I'm wearing my mom's old University of Massachusetts T-shirt and I'm sitting at the kitchen table banging away on the computer keys. How's this for a letter of introduction?

Hi!

My name is  *Trudy Walker* and I'm the person you're looking for! **No one else** in the entire universe could produce a **better**, more entertaining show than . . .

(Nah, too much. How about this:)

PLEASE, PLEASE, PLEASE pick my tape!!!!!

(Too desperate. Maybe this:)

`To whom it may concern:`

(Bag that one.)

I've been working on the proposal for two weeks now. When Denise asks me what it's about, I tell her I can't talk about it because I don't want to jinx it. She thinks I'm crazy putting this much time into something that's not a sure thing. But if there's one thing I've learned from growing up with Eddie, it's that there's *no* such thing as a sure thing. So I just keep working, making the proposal a little better every day. The problem is, I'm falling asleep by one o'clock in the afternoon, smack in the middle of Mr. Taylor's science class.

As I leave the classroom, he asks me how things are at home. It's such a perfect setup, I can't help myself.

"Things are pretty bad," I say. "My father just got back from Africa with a really bad case of malaria. Now my mother has it. I'm doing all the cooking and laundry and taking care of my brother."

Mr. Taylor's not buying it. "So you won't mind if I call her and see how she's doing."

I stick with what I've got. "She's too sick to come to the phone. Plus, the phone company disconnected us since I forgot to pay the bills on time."

"Trudy . . ."

"Yes, Mr. Taylor?"

"Trudy . . ."

I could probably stand here and play verbal seesaw with him all day, but he *is* one of the nicest teachers in the school and I'd hate to alienate him. Instead I tell him the top-secret idea for my cable show. He cleans his glasses with his out-of-style tie while he listens, then tells me he'd be glad to help me with the demo tape if I need it. I thank him and then hurry off to math.

When I get there, Ms. Ramone is talking about how many miles east a train has to go at seventy-five miles an hour to get to its destination by three o'clock. But the only problem I'm trying to solve is how I'll leave my handprints in the cement on Hollywood Boulevard without making a mess. I trace the outline of my hand on the cover of my math notebook, ✋ but when I look up, Ms. Ramone is standing next to me. I smile sweetly and tell her I was trying to visualize the problem with the train. She makes me go to the board and work the problem out for the class. She's definitely not getting tickets to the opening of my show.

Math Problems *Not* in My Textbook

1. If a woman drops an ice-cream sundae from the top of a ten-story building, what will hit the ground first—the vanilla ice cream, the hot fudge, the whipped cream, or the cherry? And if a little boy stands on the sidewalk, will he get splattered with the debris or be able to salvage a few bites?

2. Twelve people are sitting in a darkened movie theater. If one girl keeps talking during the movie, what are the chances that the other eleven people will throw their popcorn at her? And how many kernels will hit the screen before the manager comes and throws everyone out?

3. If a girl talks her mother into buying her a pair of earrings in a department store, then takes the escalator to the second floor, losing one bead of the earring on each of the revolving metal steps, what are the chances her mother will buy her anything else that day?

Private Time with Eddie

Sometimes, the best part of the day is when I'm alone with Eddie. In that time between getting ready for bed and actually going to sleep, we usually go into his room and read. No television, no video camera, no computer. I love reading to Eddie because I can make lots of mistakes or even make up a whole new story and he doesn't mind (unlike Ms. Hinchey, who stops you whenever you mess up). In fact, Eddie prefers it if you change the story every time, for variety. Better yet, he changes the story for you. If you've never heard his version of *Little Red Riding Hood*, you're missing something.

I think the reason I like this part of the day so much is that I let my mind slow down. Usually, I'm thinking about homework and television shows and soccer practice, but with Eddie, I can just relax. My mother does yoga and she says being with Eddie is like a walking meditation.

"Do you like this picture?" I ask him.

He nods.

We go through the book, a picture at a time, hardly talking, just looking. I shut the book and we just sit there, enjoying each other's company. My mother says if people just slowed down and enjoyed life more, there wouldn't be so many problems. But I'm not thinking about that now. I'm not thinking about anything except my twin brother in his inside-out pajamas smiling at me, making up stories.

Hey, John Steinbeck, Thanks a Lot

Ms. Hinchey is making us read *Of Mice and Men*. Sure enough, twenty-five pairs of eyes are glued on me. As if Eddie would ever squish a puppy or even kill somebody.

"Ms. Hinchey?" Miggs asks. "Was Lennie evil or just plain retarded?"

I raise my hand. "Ms. Hinchey, do you think people who ask dumb questions are ignorant or just trying to get attention?"

Miggs is unfazed. "Ms. Hinchey, did the rabbit have big, floppy ears or the kind that stick out like Falsie Walker's?"

"Enough, you two!" Ms. Hinchey then makes us turn to chapter seven. For the rest of the discussion, I doodle on my notebook. A rabbit with tiny ears and wings, flying out of its cage.

I wish I could ♣ Miggs.

My Final List of Things to Do

1. Interview Dr. O'Connell, pediatrician.

2. Edit the tape on the VCR.

3. Take Mr. Taylor up on his offer to help me dub music in the background.

4. Create a logo for the show—something bright, maybe a rainbow with big ears.

5. Print the proposal on Mom's color printer.

6. Make a self-addressed stamped envelope for their response.

7. Add a personal plea at the end of the videotape telling them why they should choose my tape. (They didn't ask for this but I think it may help.)

8. Wait for the cable company's decision.

I would love to tell you about my demo tape but it's TOP SECRET. (Not really; I'm just too excited to write about it.) All I can say is that it's—

AWESOME!

AMAZING!

ASTOUNDING!

(and those are just the *a*'s)

Eddie Typing on My Mother's Computer

a;wpietujfgnvlxkvm a;pwoeirft ;prjnbld,mkfc pwo
i3erfjk;dvlkc malsejfm/l;,dmv ao2wiucklx,.vnshgp
o34i5poejygm;dlkmfpwoejfpaoel;fmaw;seldjfvskh
nk,maueou5rka,nsjouwgnueauj'podgi340opjgdfcm.

(I know it looks like a lot of gibberish, but there
really is a word in there, maybe a few. And gnu is a
word we don't use enough, anyway.)

♥♥♥♥♥♥♥♥billymeier♥♥♥♥♥♥♥♥♥♥♥♥♥♥

(Aren't you curious
to find out what
my show's about?)

(At least a little?)

(Sorry,
but you'll have to wait
like everybody else.)

Things I Think About When I'm Bored (But I Hardly Have Time Anymore)

1. Sometimes I think about a woman holding a box of cereal, and on the box she's holding there is a picture of another woman holding a box of cereal, and on *that* box there is a picture of a woman holding a box of cereal, and on *that* box there is a picture of a woman holding a box of cereal . . .

2. I think about how stupid those kids in *The Sound of Music* look running around the countryside wearing clothes made out of old curtains.

3. I think about accepting an Academy Award for Best Picture, and all the people I will thank, and all the people I'll forget on purpose.

4. I think about if Eddie were a cartoon character he would be a cross between the Tasmanian

Devil and Goofy, laughing while he makes a giant mess.

5. I think about my father wandering around in circles in the jungles of Kenya, lions and gorillas at his heels. (I wonder if he thinks about me and Eddie.)

6. Sometimes, while Mr. Manning is addressing us at assemblies, I try to picture him in an evening gown, carrying a dozen roses like they do on the Miss America pageants my mother never lets me watch.

7. I imagine how easy it could have been for me to be the one with special needs. Then I wonder if Eddie would hang out with me or just leave me at home and go out with his friends instead. Denise says I got gypped because having an older brother is usually the best way to meet guys. I think about Eddie coming home with a gorgeous new kid from school who falls madly in love with me. But when I really stop to think about it, I *have* met a lot of boys and girls through Eddie, because he talks to anyone, thinking they're all his friends. Most of the time they end up to be.

social skills

The Critics Give a Big Thumbs-Down 👎
(A painful entry for me to write)

"Are you for real?" Denise asks. "A medical show? Who *cares*?" She sits down and points to the TV. "Put it in."

I cross my fingers behind my back, hoping this will be the most riveting half hour of television she's ever seen. The film begins with some instrumental guitar music, then fades into an interview with Dr. O'Connell, our pediatrician. He gestures with his hands while he speaks about asphyxia and then genetics. When I look over at Denise, she rolls her eyes.

I have edited in footage from the Special Olympics Games last summer, which shows Eddie running the 50-meter. At the end, I summarize all the important developments in the field while Eddie plays soccer behind me. My voice fades out and the guitar music fades in.

When it's over, Denise looks at me with a kind expression. I know something is wrong right away.

"You meant really well," she says. "But it's kind of . . ."

Here comes the bomb.

"It's kind of borrrrrrrrrrrrring. Who wants to see some bald-headed doctor talk about DNA? It's like hanging out with Mr. Taylor in your spare time. Couldn't you at least have found a hunky doctor?"

"I want to address an important issue," I say. "Not make some stupid version of *General Hospital*." But the sick feeling in my stomach isn't from being rejected by my friend. It stems from the fact that even *I* think the show is boring. I hate to admit Denise is right.

When I show it to my family, my mother is very enthusiastic. "I think whoever watches the show will get a lot of good information."

"*If* they watch the show," I add. "Maybe not everyone shares my interest in the subject. Not everyone likes medical documentaries."

Eddie hits the rewind button, then the fast-forward. Rewind, fast-forward.

"I hope you're not blaming yourself for Eddie's condition again," she says, sitting next to me on the couch, "and trying to make up for it by becoming an expert on the subject."

I twirl the fringe of the pillow. "I just want

people to understand him a little better, that's all." He is still pushing the buttons of the VCR. The images—stopping and starting, stopping and starting—drive me insane. I scream at him to stop.

I finally ask my mother to be honest. "Do you think it's too boring?"

"Let me put it this way, it might not be everyone's cup of tea," Mom answers.

"Thanks, a cliché always helps."

"Okay, how about this? It might not be the kind of program they're looking for if they want to attract a wide audience. Is that better?" Mom asks.

Better than what? Starting over? I ask Eddie what he thinks.

"Cowboys," he says. "And police."

He doesn't need to explain; I know what he means. Action. He's right.

"What about *The Trudy Walker Show*? I always liked that idea," my mother says. "I'll be glad to help you."

I shake my head. "Forget it. Having a cable show is a stupid idea, anyway."

"You're wrong," she says. "It's a great idea." She makes a thumbs-up sign like one of those movie critics. ☝ I turn her hand so the thumb points down. 👇 Loser. I don't need self-esteem lessons, I need get-a-life lessons. I pop the tape out of the

VCR and shove it under the cushion of the couch. I sit there for the next hour as uncomfortable as the Princess and the Pea, watching stupid sitcoms and laughing really loudly.

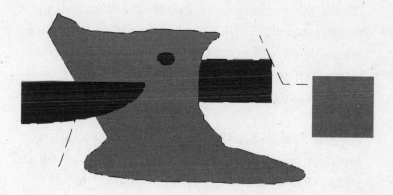

Back to square one
—Eddie Walker

Hasty Show Ideas

- A talk show where I prance around the studio audience waving a microphone in everyone's face, asking their opinions on silly topics like teenage stamp collectors with sleeping disorders or math teachers with eczema.

- A game show like *Jeopardy*, except all the questions on the board are in hieroglyphics ($\Psi\Omega\varphi\lambda\theta\Xi\varpi$) and the contestants are dressed like Egyptians.

- A soap opera for teenagers. Really melodramatic story lines of kids backstabbing each other for positions on the softball team, then coming home to find out both their parents were adopted. Lots of fake crying and surprise looks.

- HELP!!!!!!!!!!!!!!!

A Perfect Moment

During Saturday's soccer game, I try to forget my troubles and just play. Maybe someone will kick me in the head and I'll get an idea that's good for a change.

Eddie and I play on the same unified team. That means some of the kids have special needs, some don't. Eddie and I are strikers; we try to take the ball down the field to get a goal. I led the team in goals last year, Eddie led the team in assists. The way Eddie's playing this year, it might be the other way around.

Our coach, Mr. Ford, says that Eddie is a natural. He sometimes needs to be reminded not to use his hands, but he's only been whistled at a few times for that. It seems as though Eddie gets this beat going in his head—like some crazy Brazilian music—and you can't stop him. It must be a combination of how much we practice in the backyard and the fact that we are twins, because I don't even have to look to see if Eddie is open when I pass. I can sense it. My foot kicks; Eddie's receives.

We are playing one of the other neighborhood leagues and we are down 2–1. Even though people are yelling from the sidelines and Coach Ford is shouting instructions, Eddie is in that zone where all he thinks about is the ball. Every now and then I really envy the way his mind works; it doesn't get cluttered up with too much information like mine does. Eddie has no choice but to simplify. Mom says he's lucky that way.

Mike Souza passes me the ball and I start running upfield, with Eddie alongside me. Marjorie, the goalie, blocks most of the net and I know only a perfect shot to the left corner can get by her. Eddie must be reading my mind because something inside me says, "Now," and I pass him the ball. Just like in the movies, everything slows down. The ball skirts across the field and Eddie catches it beautifully inside his left foot, in what seems like slow motion. Even the crowd noises seem dull and far away. Eddie shoots the ball into the far corner, but before it leaves his foot, I know it's going in. Everyone stops—on the field, in the stands—everyone but poor Marjorie, who jumps a good two feet trying to stop it. But nothing is stopping this missile and she knows it.

The entire team is jumping up and down and

screaming; Eddie slaps me five. It is one of those pure moments when everything is just the way it should be, Eddie's handicap and all.

Coach Ford tells us there's still ten minutes to go and the score is tied. But it doesn't matter to me—or certainly to Eddie—whether we win or not. That's one of the reasons I like soccer; sometimes a tie is just as good as a win.

Dreams and Nightmares I've Had

One time I dreamt that I was parachuting into the middle of that poppy field in *The Wizard of Oz*, but instead of falling asleep, I started running toward the castle. The monkeys that usually guard the witch were all wearing seat covers and carrying ashtrays. They didn't chase me because I could fly, too, so they gave up and went to play chess.

Another time I had a dream that scared me so much I woke up screaming and my mother ran into the room to comfort me. I was on the top of the house with the woman who volunteers in the school library on Wednesdays, Mrs. Withrow. She was nailing my sneakers to the roof so I couldn't come in, and when it started to rain she put a key in my hand and climbed down. I was screaming that I was going to get electrocuted but no one could hear me.

(Note: This was the same week that we studied Ben Franklin in school.)

In my new nightmare, I'm standing in front of the entire school in the gym. The other kids don't have faces, and they are holding video cameras. They're taping every move I make and repeating everything I say like Denise does sometimes. I yell, "Stop it!" and hundreds of kids yell, "Stop it!" I say, "Cut it out!" and they say, "Cut it out!"

The best dream I ever had was when I dreamed that Eddie and I were at the beach all day—no clouds, perfect weather, and no sand sticking to us. We walked all the way home eating Popsicles that didn't melt. When I got back, I took a shower for three hours (from four to seven, according to the clock in my dream). When I woke up, I didn't want to be in the real world yet, so I went back to sleep. Even though it was morning, I dreamt I was standing under a black sky with millions of stars hanging so low I could touch them. I held the stars in my arms, spun them on my fingers like tops, then threw them in the air like leaves. When my mother finally dragged me out of bed, I was mumbling something about a celestial yo-yo.

Once I had a dream that it was just me, without Eddie. In my dream, I went through the day without worrying about him, with that part of my mind that is usually tuned to Eddie's frequency shut off. I woke up, surprisingly refreshed, but I felt guilty when I saw Eddie at breakfast.

Idea Number Two

I am still completely depressed that the deadline is a little over a week away and I have no demo tape. So much for dreams coming true and all that nonsense.

Tonight, Mrs. Hannah is coming over since my mother is going away on a business trip. Mom hates to call it baby-sitting because we're not babies, so she calls Mrs. Hannah our overnight friend. Mrs. Hannah has gray and brown hair and always wears her shirts outside her pants because she says tucking them in makes her look fat. Well, she *is* kind of fat, and bringing over a chocolate and raspberry torte every time she comes probably doesn't help.

Mrs. Hannah arrives with her cake and floral luggage. She reheats the chicken stir-fry Mom has left and then asks us if we want to play any games. Big mistake.

"Monkey Man!" Eddie says. "Let's play Monkey Man."

I feel a little cheated because that is our private

game; we've been playing it for as long as I can remember. But the thought of seeing Mrs. Hannah chasing us around the house screaming like a monkey might be worth it. I dig out the video camera.

"Monkey Man." Mrs. Hannah smiles. "Is that a nice quiet game like Monopoly?"

"Kind of," I answer. I send Eddie to the garage for props.

He returns with an old sheepskin seat cover that used to belong to my father and a pith helmet my mother wore one year for Halloween. Luckily, there are a few bananas in the bowl on the table. Sometimes, if my mother hasn't gone shopping in a while, we have to play without the bananas. I place the pith helmet on Eddie's head.

"Tru, you need a hat," he says. "Hat. Need a hat."

I take the plastic colander from under the counter and put it on.

"This game looks a little wild," Mrs. Hannah says, clapping her hands.

"Oh no," I say. "The jungle we pretend to be in is a very quiet one."

Eddie, Mr. Perfect Timing, turns on the stereo full blast, trying to find the music we always listen to when we play. It's one of the albums my father sent back from Africa when he still wrote to us.

The music is fast, with a lot of drums, and we turn it up loud.

"What do I do?" Mrs. Hannah looks so willing to please, I think about letting her be one of the explorers. But Eddie is already running around the kitchen table, gathering up speed.

I strap the sheepskin seat cover on her back and hand her two bananas. "Now you have to start screaming and chase us." I steady the camera, then hit record.

"Wouldn't you kids like to play a nice board game instead? Or maybe some cards?"

"The Monkey Man's going to get us!" Eddie shouts.

Mrs. Hannah walks toward him. "I'm going to get you!" she says sweetly.

"No, no," I say. "Like this." I hunch down and drag my knuckles on the ground. "AAAAAAAAA-AAAAAAAARGGGGGGGGGGGGGGGGH!"

Eddie starts screaming and runs into the living room.

Mrs. Hannah puts the bananas on the table. "I don't think I'll be too good at this game."

"No, you'll be great," I say. "A natural."

She smiles, then beats her hands on her chest. "Aaargh."

It takes Mrs. Hannah a while to get warmed up, but after she does she really gets into it. She takes off her shoes and runs around the house in her stockinged feet, waving the bananas and screaming. She rests for a few minutes, still wearing the sheepskin, and eats one of the bananas. She looks small and animal-like inside the black-and-white world of the viewfinder. When she starts chasing us again, she throws the peel on the floor so Eddie and I can pretend to trip on it and slide across the kitchen floor. Eddie hides in his usual spot, behind the coatrack, but starts crying when Mrs. Hannah doesn't find him fast enough.

Later, when she puts us to bed, I lay awake, rubbing the fur of the seat cover, thinking about my father in a tent, maybe surrounded by real monkeys. When the house is dark and quiet, I jump out of bed, grab the video camera, and head to the living room. Mrs. Hannah is asleep on my mother's bed.

I rewind the footage I taped and play it. The camera work is bumpy and off-center, but it complements the mood of the game. Eddie runs around the house screaming and Mrs. Hannah looks like a large animal let loose in the kitchen. Suddenly, the real Mrs. Hannah is standing behind me.

"Trudy, what are you doing?" Her hair is set in pink rubber curlers.

"Mrs. Hannah, will you do something for me?"

She nods and yawns at the same time.

"Will you sign a release form saying I can use this tape of you?"

She nods yes without asking why and heads back to bed.

Sometimes the best ideas are the ones you don't plan and make lists about. Here was my show, right in front of me. I could give out information about Eddie without a long and boring lecture. I would show his daily life like that *Real World* show on MTV. I pop out the tape and go back to bed. But I can't sleep. I keep thinking about all the things I could tape Eddie doing. Plus, I can edit in some of the home movies I already have.

The next morning, I am so excited, Eddie and I take turns jumping from the couch to the chair, pretending the rug between them is full of alligators.

"I don't think you should jump on the furniture," Mrs. Hannah says, still in her robe and matching slippers.

"We do this all the time," I lie. "It's good for Eddie's coordination."

"Coach Ford says I'm a natural," Eddie boasts.

We tell Mrs. Hannah that my mother stops at the bakery on the way to school every Friday to buy us warm brownies for our lunches. She doesn't believe us, but lets us take five Oreos apiece instead. I hide the video camera in my backpack so I can film Eddie on the bus.

"Tru's going to make me a star," he tells Jerry, who is sitting next to him. Who knows, maybe he's right.

"You're a better Monkey Man than Mrs. Hannah," Eddie tells me in the schoolyard later.

"I know. She's too fat to really chase us." I pack the camera back in my bag.

He shakes his head. "You make better monkey noises."

I give him a big "Aaaaaaaaaaaaaaaarggggggh," then head to class.

Things I Am *Almost* Too Embarrassed—
or Feel Too Guilty About—
to Enter in My Journal

1. The time after my last Girl Scout meeting when I was talking to two girls in front of Mrs. Jameson's house and Eddie walked by with Jerry. Marlene didn't know he was my brother and she started making fun of him. Eddie was at the bottom of the street and didn't see us. I laughed with her and even imitated him myself. Everyone laughed and Marlene even touched my arm, telling me to stop or she was going to have a heart attack from laughing so hard. That night I told Mom that Girl Scouts was silly and that Mrs. Jameson made us do stupid things like make wreaths out of dry macaroni. Mom said I could quit if I wanted to and I did. When I saw Marlene at school the next day, she imitated Eddie again. I pretended to smile, then hurried into science class.

2. The time last year when I really, really wanted a new CD and I didn't have any money, so I took

Eddie to the record store and showed him the one I wanted and then walked away. He picked it right off the shelf and followed me outside. I tried the plan another time with a pair of earrings, but the manager came out behind Eddie. I ran over and started yelling at Eddie that Mom was going to kill him. The man started sweating and stuttering, took the earrings back, and told us to forget about it. I felt bad that Eddie was nervous on the way home, so I played invisible Monkey Man with him to calm him down.

3. How sometimes I wish I was an only child with no twin and no "special" brother. Then I could walk to Friendly's for an ice cream and not worry about leaving Eddie behind. And how I wonder what's going to happen when we grow up, if I'll end up going to the prom with Eddie because I'll feel so bad going without him (or if I'll go with him because no one asks *me*).

4. How I walk down Corey Street even though it's a dead end just to see if I can spot Billy Meier in his yard.

5. The fact that underneath all my showbiz talk, I really would be petrified to stand in front of a studio audience.

A Natural Quality

Now that I know what I'm doing for my demo tape, I carry the video camera with me everywhere, careful not to miss a shot. With any other person, it would be difficult to be spontaneous with someone videotaping your every move, but not with Eddie. We directors call that a "natural quality." Sure, he hams it up every once in a while, but most of the time he's in that private world of his, oblivious to the camera.

I put the camera on the tripod to tape us at dinner, and stand outside the bathroom while Eddie brushes his teeth. (The station will be getting lots of mail for showing a horror film during prime time.) Mom tapes us while we play soccer and Mr. Taylor lets me leave science a few minutes early to tape Eddie and his class during recess. The tape has a kind of raw quality that I like. Denise says even if she didn't know us, she'd watch the whole show without flipping channels.

I try to call up any undiscovered twin super-powers to see if Eddie has a clue as to what I'm doing. Again I draw a blank. The only comment he makes is when I play the tape and he watches himself as if he were on a real TV show. *"Home Improvement!"* he says, and then he sits down to watch himself on screen peeling an orange. I film him watching himself on TV, watching himself on TV, watching himself on TV . . .

What Eddie Is Thinking—Maybe

!!!!!!!!!!!!!!!!!!!!!!!!! Why are all these people moving so fast? What's the hurry?

Get that camera out of my face!

!!!!!!!!!!FIRE!!!!!!!!

GOOOOOOOOOOOAAAAAALLLLLLL!

When will my mother buy me shoes that tie?

Why is my sister wearing that old seat cover and chasing me?

How old am I?

Why does everyone call me Eddie?

Words I Hate

toast

hanky-panky (one word or two?)

aluminum

pessimism

salve

camouflage

puncture

retard

A Little-Known Fact

Did you know that sometimes baby sharks will devour one another while they're still in the womb? Fighting to their death before they're even born? Mr. Taylor told us this in class today. Half the class was saying cool, the other half was saying gross, but I was silent. Maybe that's what I did to Eddie. Maybe I'm some kind of mutant shark person who thrashed and fought in the womb, trying to kill my twin, but instead just ended up handicapping him.

After class, I hang around Mr. Taylor's desk to ask him about this possibility, but I quickly feel ridiculous and leave. The theme from *Jaws* echoes in my mind. I shove my head inside my locker to make it go away. Mr. Manning, the principal, asks me why I'm still in the hall. I try to explain, but he makes me sit on the bench outside his office until I calm down. Which will probably be never.

Message on the Net for Me

deedee: Keep those messages coming, **trued**. You always brighten my day. ☺

(The smiley face is totally goofy, but it *is* nice to be liked by someone who has never even met you.)

Geography Night

Sometimes my mother gets these ideas that she wants to try out on us. The backgammon tournament ended with Eddie flushing five of his pieces down the toilet—an unsuccessful event even by Walker family standards. But Geography Night has lasted for almost two months, a lifetime around here.

At the beginning of each week, the three of us choose a country as a theme. We read up on the culture, make props, then on Friday night we cook an authentic meal. Last week was Brazil, so Eddie and I wore our soccer uniforms and ate linguica sandwiches. Eddie's shirt is permanently stained orange from the sausages.

Since this week's topic is Australia, I interview Mr. Marshall, the pharmacist, who used to live there. Eddie cuts out pictures from the old encyclopedia Mom got at a yard sale for three dollars. He makes a collage with an emu, a shark, and the real Tasmanian Devil. (Maybe this will get Mom thinking about cartoon characters and she'll remember that we still want to go to Disney World.) We cook shrimp on the barbie—outside on the grill—and talk in these weird accents that sound British. I film everything for the demo tape.

"Since Australia is surrounded by water, shall we go to the beach?" Mom asks.

I figure this means sitting in the old sandbox again with the sprinkler on. I appreciate her sense of adventure, but sometimes the end result is a little embarrassing. "Nah, we don't have to," I answer.

"Yes!" Eddie says. "The beach, the beach."

"Let's go, mates," she says. "For real this time."

Mom pulls out her straw bag, already packed with towels, a bottle of juice, and a stack of cups. Before I can say "Great Barrier Reef," we are in the car and heading south.

Because it's forty-five minutes away, we hardly ever go to the beach in the evening. When we get there, the waves are howling. We spread out the blanket Mom keeps in her trunk, holding down the edges with our sneakers. She has even packed a kite, so we run up and down the shore, screaming in our crazy Australian voices, trying to keep it in flight. I give the video camera to a man walking his dog and he films us running in the sand.

On the way home, we sing the Kookaburra

Song, because the kookaburra is a bird from the Australian bush. Eddie falls asleep before we get home and I cover him up with my towel.

When we get back, my mother carries Eddie inside as if he's a baby. Her strength surprises me. She was quiet on the drive home and as I brush my teeth I figure out why. April 19, today, is the anniversary of my grandmother's death. I guess spending time at the beach with people you love is as good a way as any to remember her spirit. I'm not sure if bringing it up will make my mother feel worse, so I don't. Instead, I climb into bed and put my arm around her. The smell of the salt makes me sad, a combination of the sea and her tears.

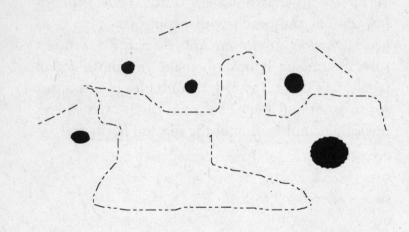

**Grandma; I miss you
—Eddie Walker**

Whew!

Finished! I'm still kind of superstitious with this tape, especially now that it's new and improved. I haven't shown it to Denise, my mom, or even Eddie. Straight to the judges at the cable company. (It's hard to use the keyboard with your fingers crossed.)

You know how when you mail a letter, you open the lid a few times afterward, just to make sure the letter goes down into the mailbox? Well, since I have to take the demo tape (references, outline, and essay included) to the post office, I don't have the opportunity to check and recheck the way I like. The guy behind the counter weighs it, sticks on the postage, and tosses it into a huge basket of mail. That's my brother's life on that tape, and hours of my hard work. The woman behind me nudges me to get out of the way; she's breathing down my neck like some kind of dragon in a sweatsuit, but I stay firmly in place. The postman smiles and tells me my package is safe and to run along. Run along? I'm not some five-year-old who's going to skip out of the post office singing tra-la-tra-la-la. I ask him for a receipt just so the monster woman behind me has to wait even longer. I know it sounds like I'm being obnoxious, but mailing the tape released a lot of bottled-up energy.

For the rest of the afternoon, I feel like Wendy from Peter Pan, flying around the sky in her night-gown. I beat Miggs to the ball in soccer practice, which I usually can't do, and finish my algebra without wincing once. (Say that three times fast.) Eddie must notice that I'm in a good mood because he asks to borrow my bike. Not only do I say yes, I volunteer to help him clean his pit of a room. When my mother tells me not to count my chickens before they hatch, I don't even yell at her for using another cliché. I just shove my hands into my armpits and flap around the kitchen like a chicken, clucking as loud as can be. I wouldn't even care if Billy Meier saw me.

I'm done!

Love Stinks
(Get ready for this one)

It's a gorgeous Sunday afternoon, so Mom, Eddie, and I go to the Charles River Festival in Cambridge. There are booths of fried dough, pottery, jewelry, even a puppet show and bands. My mother is talking to some friends and Eddie and I are wandering around the food stalls when suddenly I notice he is wearing a New York Yankees hat.

"Did Mom just buy that for you?" I ask.

He shakes his head, back and forth, back and forth.

"Well, where did you get it?"

He points to the benches near the Charles. "Some guy, Tru. Some guy."

Not again. I can't begin to count how many times I've had to apologize for something Eddie has taken. I grab his hand and drag him toward the river.

I expect some poor six-year-old to be crying

about his missing hat like the last time we were at Faneuil Hall. Or some mother telling me to just go ahead and keep the hat, her son really didn't want it, as if Eddie were going to contaminate her precious kid's hat. But what I find is a million times worse.

Billy Meier.

He is facing the water with two of his friends, Joey and Umberto. I take a deep breath and approach them, pretending Billy really knows who I am.

"Uhm, hi," I say. "Did one of you guys lose this?" I snatch the hat from Eddie's head and hand it to Billy.

He throws the hat on the ground. "I told him he could have it," Billy says. "It's Be-Kind-to-Retards Week, isn't it?" His two friends laugh. "Besides," Billy continues, "who wants a hat the three of us peed on, anyway?"

"What?! And Eddie was wearing it? You make me sick. All of you."

"What are you, baby-sitting or something? Why do you care?"

"He's my brother," I say, annoyed that Eddie chooses this exact moment to start drooling on his Celtics jacket. "My twin."

"Well, that explains it," Billy says.

"Explains what?"

"I always knew there was something special about you," he says.

"You did?" My mother would kill me with her bare hands for answering such a lamebrain, but maybe deep down Billy *was* interested in me.

"Something *really* special." He leans forward and touches my chin. "If you're twins, then you're probably retarded, too."

Roaring with laughter, his two friends raise their hands, high fives all around. I want to jump into the Charles, die from hepatitis and have my body wash up onshore so Billy gets blamed for the murder. The worst part is, Eddie is laughing, too. I grab Eddie by the arm and walk away.

"My brother may have special needs," I call over my shoulder, "but at least he's not ignorant, rude, or cruel."

"Have you checked out the booths at the fair? One of them has a great selection of rattles and baby toys." While he's talking, Billy walks across the top of the bench as if it's a balance beam.

I know it's wrong, but I run to the bench and push him with all my might. He falls to the ground and I turn around and run.

My mother has been looking for us and is annoyed when we finally find her. But as soon as she sees my face, she stops being mad and starts being worried. "What happened?"

"Trudy pushed a guy off the bench," Eddie laughs. "Wham! Right over."

I want to kill Eddie for putting me in this situation to begin with. I tell him to shut up and then I tell my mother what happened.

Her forehead is as pleated as the living room drapes. "First, let's go find out if that boy is okay," she says.

"If he's okay?" I scream. "I hope he split his head open!"

"We'll make sure he's not hurt, then you can apologize."

"*Me* apologize?"

"Just because he was a jerk doesn't mean you can be one, too."

"*No!* He peed in Eddie's hat, he told me I was retarded." I can't stop crying. Why did we have to come to this stupid festival, anyway?

She puts down her tote bag and kneels. She rocks back and forth on her knees, stroking my hair, telling me everything will be okay. When I finally stop crying and she gets up, the knees of her jeans are splattered with mud.

"Do you feel well enough to go over there?" she asks. "Or do you want me to go?"

"That would be even worse!" Of course she's not letting me off the hook. She walks the two of us toward the road.

"Remember those exercises we did?" she asks as we walk. "I want you to take some deep breaths and picture yourself strong and powerful at the top of that mountain."

Eddie begins taking deep breaths and coughing.

"She's talking to *me*," I tell him. I picture myself in New Hampshire, my feet firmly planted on the nose of the Old Man in the Mountain.

Billy, Joey, and Umberto are sitting on the bench, throwing rocks into the river. "He's fine," I tell my mother. "We can go now."

My mother shooes me toward the bench.

"I'm sorry I pushed you," I whisper into the collar of my jacket.

"Excuse me?" Billy cups his hand to his ear.

"I'm sorry," I say. "But you asked for it." My mother won't be happy with this part of the apology, but too bad.

"I missed the cement base by a few inches," he says. "Lucky for you I have perfect athletic reflexes."

I turn around to leave.

"Besides, it gets boring picking on the handicapped. Not enough of a challenge."

Walk away, I tell myself. Get out while you're ahead, with some dignity. I picture myself on top of the Mass. Ave. bridge, the sun shining on me now, not on Billy's crooked smile.

When I reach my mother, she puts her arm

around me and squeezes. Sometimes if people pick on Eddie, she steps in and tells them they are acting out of ignorance, that Eddie is a lot like them if they'd take the time to notice. But because it's Billy Meier, she zips her jacket and starts walking toward the car. I know if I ask for a candied apple, she'll say yes and she does.

On the way home, I remember an old album from her college days that Eddie used to play. There is a song on it, "Love Stinks," and I start to hum it in the car. My mother laughs when she recognizes it, but thankfully, she doesn't say anything about Billy. If I add up all the time I have wasted thinking about going out with him, or having him come to one of my soccer games, I'd have enough time to film two feature-length movies. I can't figure out which of us is the bigger loser. When I get my own show, he'll have to stand outside for three days and two nights in the rain to wait in line for tickets and even *then* he won't get in.

But Eddie . . . Eddie is oblivious. (I wish I could be sometimes.) He rolls down the window, paying attention only to the cherry blossoms on Memorial Drive and the crisp spring wind blowing off the river.

Graffiti on the wall of the second-floor girls' bathroom:

Billy Meier
eats hell

(I have *no* idea who wrote this . . .)

Soup or Sandwich?

It's a Saturday morning and Denise, Eddie, and I are watching the Three Stooges. Eddie is running his usual commentary: Every time someone picks up a hammer, Eddie says, "He's picking up the hammer," and before the clanging noise begins, Eddie's already yelling, "Ouch!" It's too bad we don't have any blind friends because they would really enjoy watching TV with Eddie.

My mother peeks into the room, rubbing her neck the way she does when she's been at the computer for a few hours. "What do you kids want for lunch?"

Denise nudges me.

"I'm not going to do it," I say.

"Come on," Denise begs.

I sigh. "Hey, Eddie," I say. "For lunch, do you want soup or a sandwich?"

"Sandwich."

I ask him again, a little differently this time. "Do you want a sandwich or soup?"

"Soup."

Eddie always picks the last thing you say, no matter what it is. "Do you want soup or a dead bird?" I ask.

"A dead bird."

Denise keeps doing it, asking him over and over, laughing at the different answers each time.

"That's no way for future women to act," my mother calls from the kitchen. Denise and I roll our eyes.

Eddie is so busy pretending to hit himself in the head that he doesn't notice that we've been goofing on him.

Later we play games on my mother's computer and help her plant tulip bulbs even though it's still drizzling. Eddie's fingernails are usually kind of dirty, anyway, but after working in the garden, all of us are filthy.

"This is how it must be in Africa where my father is," I tell Denise. "He spends a lot of time in the rain forest."

When Denise and Eddie go into the house to wash up, my mother pulls me aside.

"Tru, you know your father isn't in Africa. Why did you say that?"

I scrape the mud off the palm of my hand with my fingernail. She kneels down beside me. "We've been through this before. After he left, he spent three months in Africa, then moved to Rhode

Island. He lives in an apartment building, not a thatched hut. You know this."

Maybe it's my overactive imagination or maybe I'm a little slow, too. Or maybe the truth is too boring. Or painful. "It's more fun to pretend he's in Rwanda, not Rhode Island," I tell her.

"He didn't leave because of you," she says.

"He left because of Eddie, didn't he?"

"There were lots of reasons why he left. It wasn't one thing. How many times have I told you that? I don't want you making up any more stories, okay?"

I nod. "Why is Eddie the way he is?"

She rubs her face with her hands, leaving two brown streaks of mud. "You know why. Because the cord was wrapped around his neck and they couldn't get him out of me fast enough."

"Was it because of me? Because I was squishing him? Or thrashing around like a baby shark?"

She tilts her head, not knowing what I'm talking about. "I don't blame myself, you shouldn't blame yourself, either." She holds out the tulip bulbs in her hand. "Just like these, right? They could blossom any color. It's a surprise. Like everything in life."

I want to tell her the bag they came in said all the tulips inside were Royal Reds, but with the rain frizzing her hair and the mist around us, she looks like a fuzzy angel and I want to believe her.

We go inside and make hot chocolate. Denise calls her mother to see if she can stay, then we all make pizza for dinner. Later we sit in a circle in the living room surrounded by candles and take turns telling ghost stories. My mother's are the scariest, and Eddie tells the same one as always, about the man with the hook for a hand. Denise makes one up about a leprechaun who lures people to their death with his pot of gold. I know I can't tell my usual—a man lost in the jungles of Africa—so instead I tell one about a little girl who is knocking on apartment doors, looking for her father. Door after door opens, and no one is there, until finally someone says, "Come in." But by the time she gets inside, the person has gone, and all she finds is a sheet lying on the couch, remnants of a forgotten ghost.

Still haven't heard about my tape . . .

B.J.'s Sleepover

The pajama party at my friend B.J.'s is the first thing I've done without Eddie in months. The six of us unroll our sleeping bags in the basement (the finished part, not the cement area with the dartboard where her brother hangs out) and pass around a big glass bowl of popcorn.

The first item on the agenda for any of our sleepovers is a seance. Denise asks if she can be the Gypsy first. She wraps one of B.J.'s mother's scarves around her head and borrows my hoop earrings (say good-bye to those). B.J. empties the popcorn into a plastic container and turns the glass bowl upside down to use as a crystal ball.

We sit in a circle around Denise.

"Mr. Santos," Denise chants, swaying back and forth. "We are trying to reach you."

Mr. Santos was the old janitor at our school who died last summer from a heart attack.

"Mr. Santos, where are you?"

We all have our eyes closed and are quietly

humming. Suddenly there's a loud crash and we all jump.

"Mr. Santos!" Denise says, waving her arms. "Let us see you!"

But it's not Mr. Santos who enters the room, it's B.J.'s crazy grandmother, Nana Beauchene. She isn't really crazy, just eccentric, B.J.'s mother says. Nana squeezes into the circle between me and Judi Hedren. "I love seances," she says. "Let me give it a go."

Denise reluctantly hands over the scarf and the crystal ball. (I hold out my hand until she forks over the earrings.)

Nana Beauchene ties the scarf tightly around her head. "Alphonso," she says in a voice much lower than her usual one, "come to me."

"Alphonso," we repeat. "Come to us."

B.J. rolls her eyes and mouths the words "My grandfather."

Nana Beauchene might still be with us in body, but her mind is definitely somewhere else. She starts talking in a language I have never heard before, not even on Geography Night. By the look on B.J.'s face, she hasn't heard it before, either.

The bulkhead door begins to bang and a cool breeze blows into the cellar. "Alphonso," she says. "Play."

She sits down at the old upright piano and starts

playing, a slow waltz-type song that sounds a few hundred years old. Her eyes are still closed but she doesn't miss a note. Judi Hedren begins to cry and runs upstairs to call her mother. Suddenly the breeze stops and so does Nana Beauchene.

"He's gone now." She unties the scarf and drapes it across the piano. She pats B.J. on the head and goes upstairs.

Nice time to forget the video camera!

After she leaves the room, B.J. tells us her nana doesn't know how to play the piano, but Papa Alphonso used to play all the time. We are still kind of scared, so we watch *Clueless* for the millionth time and finish the rest of the popcorn. We take a vote to invite Nana Beauchene to the next sleepover, no matter whose house it's at. After we go to bed, I lie awake in my sleeping bag, listening to B.J. snore, watching the fringe of the scarf spread across the piano like silken fingers.

Probable Responses to the Sleepover Story If I Ever Work It into My Hit Show

Trudy completely made up the part about the grandmother. I mean, who would wreck a sleepover faster than a grandmother?

As if.

The grandmother was probably speaking Russian or something.

I'm sure Trudy hasn't seen *Clueless* a million times. It's good, but it isn't *that* good.

Do you think I could borrow Trudy's earrings?

Where's Eddie? He's more interesting.

Mom's Dates

Mom hasn't had a boyfriend in a while. She's gone on dates, sure, but usually the guy fades out pretty quickly after spending time with me and Eddie.

One guy—his *name* was Guy, but he pronounced it the French way, *Ghee*—used to take my mother to the movies on Friday nights. When they got back, he'd always act surprised that we were still up. Once, while my mother was making coffee, he offered Eddie and me five dollars to leave him and Mom alone.

Eddie grabbed the money from his hand and ran into the kitchen. "Guy gave us five dollars. Let's go to Disney World." (He was serious.)

My mother thought Guy was just being nice until I told her he was trying to bribe us. He left before the coffee was ready.

Another time, she was seeing someone she met at a business meeting in New York. His name was Peter and he used to let Eddie and me take turns driving his car in the Star Market parking lot. My mother was quiet around the house for days after he started seeing someone else.

But she must've been *really* lonely when she decided to go out with Danny. He has one of those I'm-so-cool goatees and hair so slicked back, it looks like he uses a gallon of Vaseline. He never talks to Eddie or me, he just nods as if ignoring us will make us go away. But the real reason I don't like him is the way my mother acts around him. Laughing at things that aren't funny, talking about things she doesn't care about—the way I used to act around Billy Meier before I came to my senses. I know I should respect her choices, but even the remote possibility of having Danny for a father makes my skin crawl.

I hear his car pull into the driveway. He always locks his car, even if he pops in for a minute.

Eddie is watching TV in the living room. "Hey, Eddie," I say. "Act retarded." (Completely unfair, I know. The worst, I admit it.) But for some reason, Eddie gets the idea. He limps to the front door like Quasimodo.

"Danny, hey, Danny boy. How're you doing, Danny? Hi, Danny."

I'd never ask anyone to do something I wouldn't do myself, let alone Eddie, so I join in.

"Hey, Danny old boy, old Danny, old boy, old Danny." I'm kind of spitting and crossing my eyes.

(Not that any special-needs kids I know do *either* of these things, but I am using autistic—I mean artistic—license.)

Danny tries not to stare at us and looks helplessly toward my mother. "Virginia, what's going on?"

She gives me her this-is-not-funny face, that I-know-what-you're-doing face.

"Trudy's very imaginative. She's practicing for a play."

I can't stop now. "Dannnnnnnnnnnnnny. Dannnnnnnnnnnnnnny."

She pats me on the head like a dog. "We won't be long."

The problem with getting Eddie to do any kind of acting is that it's hard to get him to stop. I spend the next twenty minutes trying to get him back to normal—whatever that means.

When my mother comes back around ten o'clock, Danny doesn't come in. She sits next to me on the couch.

"All you had to do was tell me you didn't like him. You didn't have to embarrass yourself. Or Eddie."

"Why can't you go out with a nice guy for a change?" Even before I say it, I know it's a mean thing to say. Between working and taking care of us, she doesn't have much time to meet men, never mind good ones looking for a relationship with a woman with two kids.

She suddenly looks tired and kind of old. "Maybe someday I'll be lucky enough to meet someone as perfect as Billy Meier," she says.

I want to tell my mother I'm sorry, but I don't. When she gets off the couch, her pocketbook swings from her arm and almost hits me.

A Frying Pan Hits Me on the Head—
Oh Yeah, Eddie Has Special Needs

I am so tired of pacing around the kitchen and biting my nails waiting for the cable company to call me about my tape that I decide to take Eddie to the mall on Boston Bruins Day. Mistake! The place is crawling with a million kids all wearing the same yellow-and-black jacket as Eddie, all screaming and jostling to see their favorite hockey players. I first notice that Eddie's missing in the record store. When the manager says she hasn't seen him, I run out of the store to look for him.

Suddenly I feel like a flower surrounded by hundreds of buzzing bees. Everywhere I turn there is another kid in one of those stupid yellow-and-black jackets. I grab a few of them by the arm but they're not Eddie. (One guy gets pretty mad.) An expression of my mother's comes to mind: "The squeaky wheel gets the grease." I cup my hands to my mouth like a megaphone. "Eddie Walker!"

Nothing.

In the center of the mall, a large cluster of kids

are jumping up and down, asking one of the hockey players for his autograph. I push my way through the crowd, calling for Eddie. One part of me hopes he's here, but another doesn't. If there's one thing Eddie is, it's claustrophobic. I don't need any special twin power to recognize his voice in the center of the crowd, anyone within a ten-mile radius can hear him. Thank you, angel.

The word *relief* doesn't come close to explaining the look on Eddie's face when he sees me. But his expression also shows fear and anger, and most of all, frustration. I pull him out of the crowd and into the nearest shop.

He keeps tugging at his ears and brushing his head as if to get rid of cobwebs. His body sways back and forth like some kind of monk in a trance. "Tru, Tru, Tru, Tru," he chants over and over.

"Eddie, I'm sorry. I'm sorry." We sound like Pete and Repeat. "Let's go catch the bus."

The thought of the sardine-packed city bus must have thrown him into a frenzy. He knocks over a rack of women's lacy underwear with his thrashing. Two salespeople try to usher us out the door but I tell them no. Eddie hasn't had a panic attack in years, but I know the last thing to do right now is to try and move him. "Just let it play itself out," my mother said last time. I hold him close while he wails, paying no attention to the crowd that is gathering. By the time the security guard comes, Eddie is wiped out.

The guard—a nice grandfatherly type named Emmitt—lets me call my mother to come pick us up, then he helps the women hang up the clothes Eddie has knocked over. Even though I have my hands full with Eddie, I still wonder if Emmitt is embarrassed picking up all those little silk nighties. They look much more uncomfortable to sleep in than my mom's old T-shirts.

We wait at the front entrance, next to the shop for tall men. Eddie's face is damp with sweat and spit, so I wipe it with my bandanna. I am fiddling with the zipper of my purse when I hear something that sounds like a wounded buffalo in that Kevin Costner movie. It's Eddie.

He is looking at himself in the full-length mirror, sobbing. "I don't want to be different," he says. "I want to be the same. Same as everybody else."

His wish doesn't form the lump in my throat; his self-awareness does. He has never talked about his condition before, never questioned his identity.

"Everybody's different," I say. "Not just you."

He rubs his eyes and continues to look at himself in the mirror and cry. His dark hair sticks up around his face, his green eyes are wet with grief. "No," he says. "Just like you. Just like you."

Our images in the mirror look similar—we are

twins after all—but when I look at him now, I see me, see the life I could have had if *I'd* been the one tangled in the umbilical cord.

I put my arm around him. "You're the best brother in the world," I say, trying to be sincere but sounding like some bad Hallmark card. "I wouldn't change anything about you."

He shakes my arm off, still wounded.

By the time my mother comes, we are both crying.

When she sees us, I think she might start crying, too. But by the time we get home, Eddie is quiet and goes up to his room to play records. At dinnertime he's fine, and we play Monkey Man later. But the image that keeps flashing in front of me is Eddie looking at himself in the mirror, saddened by what he sees. A lot of people don't like what they see in the mirror, but it's usually something superficial like a zit or a few extra pounds. Eddie was upset by something that he couldn't change with a flashy product or fancy diet. His best hope rests with one person—me. I'll double my efforts to come up with some kind of cure, some kind of . . . something, so the next time he stares at himself in the mirror, the reflection looking back is one he's happy to see.

I can't even believe that during my twin brother's moment of intense emotional pain, for a moment—just a moment—I cursed myself for not bringing the video camera. I am so heartless and cruel, maybe I should consider a career change. Is it too late to think about law school?

SNORE!

(I'm getting tired of waiting . . .)

A Sicko Way to Spend a Rainy Sunday Afternoon—Playing "What If?"

- What if I called Rhode Island Information? (Area code 401—I really did check.)
- And what if there was a listing for Edward Walker, Sr.?
- And what if I dialed the phone and my father answered, and I hung up really fast?
- Then what if he dialed ★69 and called me back not knowing it was me and started yelling at me for making crank phone calls?
- Then what if I told him I was his daughter and he asked me how Mom and Eddie were, and whether we got his box of African souvenirs nine years ago?
- And what if he remarried and has two pretty daughters with nice normal names like Jenny and Patti.
- And what if these two new stepsisters started torturing me for the rest of my life like I was poor Cinderella?
- And what if I asked my father if he had any

information that would help me cure Eddie and he told me Eddie was never going to change and I said, "How do you know?" and he told me I had to move on and I said, "Like you?"

· What if he hung up in a hurry and left me holding the phone, listening to the dial tone?

· And what if I took the bag of jelly beans I'm eating and hurled them up to the ceiling one by one until it looks like the ceiling's been stained with permanent confetti? What then?

(It has *got* to stop raining soon . . .)

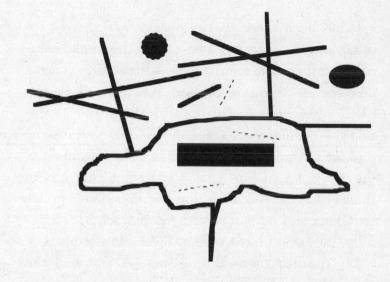

Abandoned Children
—Eddie Walker

A Patched Bot Wever Noils

It has been three weeks since I mailed my proposal and demo tape. I've called the cable company's office fourteen times—a few times using fake voices—trying to find out when they'll be finished reviewing applications. I think the receptionist recognized my voice the last time because he told me nothing had changed since the beginning of the week. I told him that was wrong, that lots of things had changed, including the President's policy on China and my substitute math teacher. (Hopefully, they don't have ★69 at the cable station . . .)

My mother keeps telling me, "A watched pot never boils." I hate it when she tries to reduce life to handy clichés like "Don't cry over spilled milk" or "That's the way the cookie crumbles." An old housewife must have made up all of these clichés a long time ago, because they all have to do with kitchens and food.

(Don't you like how my computer puts the correct accent on the e in cliché? Pretty cool, huh?)

I check my e-mail and there's a message from **deedee**, answering my last inquiry. "Your brother is very lucky to have a sister who cares so much about him," she/he says. "But I'd hate to see you wait for a cure that may not be coming. I'll let you know if I hear of anything that might make his life easier, but maybe you should concentrate on yourself for a while."

I write back and say thanks for the advice but that I'll never be happy until Eddie is cured. I go back to sitting by the phone, waiting for the cable company to call.

Eddie makes matters worse by bugging me—at least twenty times—asking me when I'll get my own show. "When do you find out, Tru? Huh? When? When, Tru? What day? When?"

"I DON'T KNOW!" I yell so loud, he blocks his ears. Why can't he be a little more patient, like me?

When I go to bed, I draw a skull and crossbones on today's date on the calendar. ☠ Stupid cable company. I don't even want a show anymore.

When I get home from school the next day, my mother hands me a piece of mail from the cable company.

The envelope, please:

Yes!

Did I say I hated them? I *love* that cable company.

What the Letter Said
(My Version)

Dear Ms. Walker (may we call you Tru?):

Congratulations!!!!!!!!! Your tape was the best tape we have ever seen. We sat through more than 200,547 tapes and yours was the only one that wasn't boring. We loved it! We can't wait to meet you and your lovely brother, Eddie. We also want you to begin taping immediately—we need a new show every week for the next five years. We know this will be a lot of work for you, but we have complete faith in your talent.

Your new best friends,
The cable company

P.S. Did we mention that we loved the tape?

What the Letter Said
(The Real Version)

Dear Ms. Walker:

Congratulations! We are proud to announce that your tape, *Real Life with Eddie*, was the winner of our community cable contest. We will contact you this week with a specific time and date to broadcast your show.

Sincerely,

Christy Morelli
Community Liaison

(Both letters kind of say the same thing . . .)

Trudy Walker

(In case you want to keep this for when I'm famous.)

What, Me? Nervous?

Just because Mr. Manning made an announcement over the P.A. system for everyone to watch the show Thursday night at seven . . . And just because there was an article in the town newspaper . . . And just because everyone is going to tell me how stupid the show was as soon as I walk into class Friday morning . . . And just because my mother invited my grandfather and Mrs. Hannah over to our house to watch the show . . . And just because I've been feeling nauseous for two days . . . And just because my face has broken out in so many zits that it looks like a Braille copy of *War and Peace* . . .

No, I'm not nervous.

I'm terrified . . .

LIGHTS, CAMERA, ACTION!

(I'm just practicing . . .)

Unhappy Birthday to You

Paula Ferrone invited Denise, Eddie, and me to her birthday party. Last year Denise was invited but not me or Eddie. We heard about it afterward, how her parents rented all these pinball machines and twenty kids played for free all afternoon while her mother passed out Cokes and popcorn. I think the only reason we're invited now is because of the TV show. I don't really care why; I just want to go.

I was wondering how they'd top last year's party, but when we arrive it's obvious: The entire house is covered in aluminum foil like a giant spaceship. A six-foot alien is taped to the front door.

Eddie runs up the steps and into the house. "Beam me up, Scotty!"

"I didn't know this was a space theme," Denise said, "or I would've gotten her meteor earrings."

"That's okay. I got her a Ouija board. She can talk to space aliens and they can answer her." I hold up the box, but all Denise is interested in is the wrapping paper. Eddie designed a wavy pattern on the computer, then my mother printed it out on the oversize printer at work. The paper is almost more interesting than the present.

Paula's mother bought all these dryer vents from Sears and hung them around the house so it looks like the guts of a spaceship. The television plays a video of the men walking on the moon, and the door to the family room is covered with dials and buttons like a giant control panel. Everyone who's been invited is running around the house going crazy with the ray guns Mrs. Ferrone handed out as party favors.

After we play Comet Escape and Star Tunnel, Paula opens her presents. She rips our present open without even looking at the paper. But Eddie doesn't notice. When she is finished with the presents, she cuts the cake (which is in the shape of Saturn, with licorice for the rings). Just as she hands me my piece, Miggs Macrides pops the balloon tied to the back of his chair. Eddie yells and I get a flashback of the mall incident.

"He's afraid," I tell Miggs. "Stop it, okay?"

Miggs looks to make sure Mrs. Ferrone is still in the living room passing out cake. "Oh, the TV star is scared?" He holds his plastic fork next to another balloon.

"Don't even think about it," I say.

When he smiles, the piece of frosting wedged

between his front teeth attaches itself to his top lip. "Sorry, Falsie," he says. "I can't control myself." He calls over two boys behind him. "We're losing pressure!" he yells, then pops the balloon. Soon everyone is grabbing balloons and popping them. Mrs. Ferrone runs in to see what is going on, but by then Eddie is covering his ears and screaming.

I grab Eddie by the arm and force him past the breaking balloons into the backyard. We run through the Ferrones' yard and into the neighbor's. I hold on to Eddie until he stops, then sit him down in the red wagon near the swing set. Mrs. Ferrone, Paula, and Denise follow us, all apologetic, but I tell them we're fine. They go back to the party for the grand finale.

"Are you okay?" I ask.

He covers his ears. "So loud!"

I hug him again. "I know. I'm sorry."

He runs his hand across the side of the wagon. "Pull me?"

"Eddie, you're too old for that."

"Please?"

As I pull him around the neighbor's backyard, I wonder if anyone is home and will come running outside to stop us. Then I start getting mad—at Miggs, of course, but also because I'm missing the best part of the party. Mr. Ferrone is probably going to light the house on fire and sail it into the sky. When I turn around to look at Eddie, he is rocking back and forth in the wagon, trying to comfort himself. It's kind of hard to feel sorry for myself when I look at him.

I am still pulling him after the party guests leave. Denise gets a ride home with Sara, and my mother finally finds us in the neighbor's yard. She takes over pulling, and I sit in the wagon with Eddie, the three of us circling the yard like settlers on some new frontier.

Paranoid Fortune Cookies

HEY CINDERELLA - YOUR HALF SISTERS WANT THEIR FRACTIONS REDUCED

YOU ARE THE LEAST CREATIVE PERSON EVER BORN

WE'RE ALL WAITING FOR YOU TO LEAVE SO WE CAN START TALKING ABOUT YOU

EVEN THE PEOPLE WHO DIDN'T WATCH THE SHOW HAVE COMPLAINED

YOUR SHOW IS THE WORST HALF HOUR
IN TELEVISION HISTORY

YOUR BROTHER ISN'T DEVELOPMENTALLY DELAYED; YOU ARE

YOUR FATHER IS WATCHING YOUR SHOW RIGHT NOW
AND HE'S GLAD HE LEFT

IT'S SEVEN P.M. AND ALL YOUR CLASSMATES ARE VOMITING

LOSER

Headline in the *Boston Globe* Tomorrow:

TRU OR FALSE? LOCAL SHOW IS A 💣

TRU!

One Special Tulip

My mother asks me to hang Eddie's sheets on the line outside. (A few times a year he still wets the bed.) I dig the clothespins out of the bag, just happy to be outside, away from the phone and the TV. On the way back in the house, I pick some weeds from the garden. My mother's done a good job—the tulips, zinnias, and marigolds surround the tree like those floral necklaces they wear in Hawaii. Just as I turn to go, I notice one purple tulip in the midst of all the deep red ones. It's a little smaller than the others, but the color is magnificent—deep indigo, like the color of my bike. I go into the kitchen and smile at my mother. She smiles back, not knowing why I'm smiling. From the kitchen window, the purple flower shines—brighter than the quartz on Mr. Taylor's desk—while Eddie's Mickey Mouse sheets wave in the breeze.

Gulp!

The day before the show, I log onto the Net while my mother is at work. There are no messages in her mailbox, so I stare at the blank screen for several minutes. My fingers start typing way ahead of my mind. The screen continues to scroll down as I talk about the show, how nervous I am, how Eddie isn't getting any better. On the Net, I am anonymous and that gives me the freedom to really speak my mind. At the end of my spiel, my finger hovers over the keyboard. Send or delete? I do an invisible "eenie, meenie, minie, mo," but stop halfway and hit Send. People can ignore it if they want to; I'm not forcing anyone to read it.

When I check the e-mail later that afternoon, there are three messages. **Billybob** says he'll have to upgrade his hard drive if I leave any more really long messages. **Kato 2** says the Net is no substitute for a psychiatrist's couch. When I spot the message from **deedee**, I pour myself a glass of juice and sit down.

Deedee says it sounds like I have a lot on my

plate—a cliché as stupid as any of Mom's. She says it's normal to be nervous, with my friends and family making such a fuss about the show. She asks if I can enjoy my success without worrying about my brother. She wishes me luck and suggests something I haven't thought of before. She says she'll be on the Net Saturday morning at nine if I want to chat with her live. I've gone inter-active lots of times in the Trivia rooms (no one knows more about the Brady Bunch than me), but I've never really had a private conversation with someone. I leave **deedee** a message saying I'll be there.

Funny, sometimes it's something a stranger says, or something you overhear, that gets you thinking about your life. I log off the computer, wondering if my fascination with Eddie's condition has more to do with me than with him. I spend the rest of the afternoon trying to do my homework. Because Ms. Ramone got a bad haircut, she gave us seven-teen problems to do. In math, the answers are either right or wrong, never in between. Maybe that's why I don't like it; nothing else in life works that way.

The Big Night

I begged the woman at the cable company all week to let me watch the show at the studio so I wouldn't have to watch it at home. She said no. So I'm up in my room, hiding, until seven o'clock. My mother wants me to come down and be sociable with Mrs. Hannah and my grandfather, but I can't. All I want to do is crawl under my bed and cover myself in dust balls.

Mom calls me at ten of seven. I have memorized a list of excuses to use if people start saying how much the show stinks. I'll say the idea was experimental, or Eddie didn't take direction well, or the battery kept running out of the camera. Or maybe I'll just admit that I *do* stink and will never end up on television. Ten years from now, I'll be on the other side of the school lunch line, tossing mashed potatoes onto your plate with an ice-cream scooper. AAAAAAAAARRRRRRRGGGGGGGGGGG-GGHHHHHHHHH! (And I'm not even playing Monkey Man.)

Mrs. Hannah gives my hand a squeeze, and my

grandfather is smiling so wide, you'd think they just called his number for the lottery. Mom has me take a few deep breaths—o-n-e, t-w-o, t-h-r-e-e— and we settle in front of the TV. When I see Eddie, I realize I'm being a complete jerk. He's in cousin Kevin's tuxedo, holding one of my grandfather's unlit cigars, as cool and graceful as a movie star. Well, he *is* kind of a star. I decide I've been acting like a moron and try to enjoy the rest of the evening.

Ms. Morelli, the woman from the cable station, begins by talking about all the great applications they had for show ideas. A pet-trick show, a how-to-fix-your-car show, even a mime show. She says my show was chosen because it was "reality based." Mom says anyone who wants a dose of our reality is welcome to come help out anytime. When Ms. Morelli finishes, the screen goes blank. I think they might be having technical difficulties— kind of like Eddie, I guess—but a few seconds later, my image fills the screen. My mother tells me to stop complaining about how I look so she can listen. I seem pretty serious, talking about Eddie—how great he is and how I wanted to share our lives with others in the community. Then my director's chalkboard fills the screen. DAILY LIFE WITH EDDIE—TAKE ONE. (I only *do* one take, but I like clicking the chalkboard and yelling "Take

One.") On the screen, when I yell, "Action," Eddie starts running around the kitchen. He finally winds down and starts going through the cupboards. He eats a graham cracker and the crumbs are flying out of his mouth faster than spray out of a garden hose.

"Tru, really," my mother says. "What's next, picking his nose?"

"No, just some burping and farting," I say to annoy her.

Eddie keeps repeating, "I'm on TV, aren't I, Tru? That's me, right, Tru? I'm on TV. Like Gilligan."

The comparison isn't a bad one. I tell him to keep quiet while we watch.

It's strange to see the chairs you sit on every day, the curtains, the kitchen table, on TV like the set of some sitcom. When the Monkey Man episode is on, Mrs. Hannah seems a little embarrassed.

"I look so heavy," she says over and over. No one responds.

"Mrs. Bell is on TV. Look, it's Mrs. Bell," Eddie says when his teacher appears.

The show follows Eddie on a typical day—some highlights, but also some boring stuff, too—until we get to the last shot. Eddie is sitting on the front steps of our house, wearing sunglasses and his leopard-print robe, playing a harmonica. (A nice unplanned moment, if I do say so myself.) The scene fades to black, followed by the cable news.

I don't realize till after the show is over that I have twirled my hair into several little pieces that are now sticking up like a porcupine. Mom and Eddie are jumping up and screaming, and Mrs. Hannah is holding out her shirt and examining her waistline, and Grandpa is nodding back and forth, back and forth, kind of like Eddie does. I'm in a daze. Excited—yes—but also experiencing the same anticlimactic feeling I have when I stay up till midnight on New Year's Eve.

"You did it!" My mother picks me up and twirls me the way she used to when I was little. "You did exactly what you wanted to do—made an interesting show that informs people about others with special needs." It seems as if her heart is about to explode with pride. "Good for you, Tru."

Eddie tackles me and Mom doesn't say anything when we jump from the couch to the chair and back again. She still doesn't say anything when my grandfather lights Eddie's cigar and he pretends to smoke it.

The phone starts ringing immediately. Denise calls first, still angry that her mother had to work and she had to watch her little sister at home instead of being here with me. She's screaming with excitement, but the call-waiting keeps going off, so I tell her I'll call her later. I am completely shocked when I click the phone to the next caller and it's Mr. Manning.

"Trudy, I just wanted to tell you how much Mrs. Manning and I enjoyed your show."

If anyone in my class found out—especially Miggs—that the principal called me at home to say something *nice*, they'd torture me for the rest of my life. I say something humble and polite and get off the phone as fast as I can.

My mother brings out a cake she has hidden in the garage that says "Congratulations Tru and Eddie." But Eddie won't let her cut it until we all sing "Happy Birthday." I eat the cake and talk to everyone but I feel a million miles away.

In bed that night, I try to decide how I feel. Happy? Proud? Self-conscious? Something is bothering me, but I can't figure out what it is. Maybe I'm just nervous to hear the general reaction tomorrow. I wish I could be invisible (or a fly on the wall, as my mother would say), overhearing everyone in the halls, oblivious to their criticism, distanced from their opinions. One thing is for sure—Eddie was really great. Make that two things—so was I.

A Sample of Possible Reactions

I thought it was the stupidest thing I'd ever seen. I turned it off halfway through to watch one of those church stations—*that*'s how boring it was.
—*Miggs Macrides*

The camera work was good and I liked the informal tone. I think it might have been better if she'd worked in some math problems, though.
—*Ms. Ramone*

She is soooooooooooo awesome. I am completely green with envy.   —*Denise Palumbo*

Look for this film in our Top Ten Picks of the Year.   —*Siskel and Ebert*

Yeah, like I want to sit home and relax and watch some knucklehead on TV.   —*Billy Meier*

The boys won't admit it, but I overheard a few of them outside at lunch. They thought it was cool and they want to be in the next show she does.

—*B.J. Beauchene*

We need more shows like this to educate people who don't come in contact with a lot of special-need kids. I thought it was great, even though my dandruff really showed up. —*Mrs. Bell*

I can't believe I missed it! I would have given anything to see it! —*Eddie Walker, Sr.*

A cross between Woody Allen and Fellini. A documentary both surreal and realistic. A true accomplishment. —*Martin Scorsese*

Eddie is totally neat and really funny. He's the coolest kid at school.

—*general opinion of the student population*

The Next Day at School

I say, "Thanks a lot, glad you liked it," about four million times. Kids who never even said hello to me before are waiting at my locker, smiling and laughing like we're old friends. I'm sure they're thinking that if the cable company likes my tape and gives me a weekly show, maybe I'll film them and they'll be on TV, too. Yeah, well, keep thinking.

On the other hand, Eddie is absolutely basking in the attention. He talks to everyone, enjoying his celebrity status. He obviously doesn't hold grudges, because he even plays basketball with Miggs and that phony Billy Meier during recess. (Luckily, I didn't witness that sight on a full stomach.) Suddenly, everyone at school wants to be our friend.

That's really great, I guess.

My Real Reaction to the People Who Are Suddenly Being Nice

HYPOCRITES! HOW MANY OF YOU HAVE EVER HAD LUNCH WITH US, WALKED HOME FROM SCHOOL WITH US, OR CARRIED ON A MEANINGFUL CONVERSATION WITH US? HARDLY ANY OF YOU! NOW YOU'RE TRIPPING OVER YOURSELVES TO BE OUR FRIENDS. YOU MAKE ME SICK, ALL OF YOU!

(At least *pretend* to get to know us first . . .)

Trying to Sort It Out

Now that I've done all my ranting and raving, something is *still* bothering me. As much as I'd like to blame the kids at school, it's not them. It's not Eddie. It's me. I tried to talk to my mother about it, but my insides felt like a constipated volcano. She tried to listen, but I couldn't come up with anything to say. Something about watching Eddie on TV . . . Was I exploiting our life for my own stardom? Maybe. But I *did* want the viewing audience to learn more about kids like Eddie. Was it that Eddie was getting more attention than me since he was the one mostly on camera? Maybe. But I still don't think that's it. Then what's the *problem*? I rack my brain like a little Einstein . . . Maybe I should sit under a tree and wait for an apple to hit me on the head.

(Don't bother jumping on your computer to correct me; I *know* it was Newton who got hit with the fruit. Just making sure you're on your toes.)

My On-Line Conversation with Deedee

Luckily, my mother has to go into work this morning so I'm free to meet **deedee** on-line.

trued: Nine o'clock, right on time.

deedee: How was your show?

trued: Okay, I guess.

deedee: Okay? Is that all?

trued: People at school actually liked it. They're going kind of crazy.

deedee: You should be proud of yourself.

trued: I am, I guess.

deedee: You don't sound too excited. Is something wrong?

My fingers freeze on the keyboard. One word at a time.

trued: It's just that . . . I haven't really told anyone this, and I'm still not sure about it,
but for the first time, watching Eddie on
TV like that made me see him in a different way.

deedee: What do you mean?

trued: I mean, you could really tell he has special
needs.

deedee: I don't get it. Can't you always tell?

trued: It's just that watching Eddie like that was
more . . . I don't know . . . objective. He's
not going to get better. He's developmentally delayed. He's staying that way.

deedee: Deep down, didn't you always know that?

trued: No. I mean, yes. I don't know. Maybe.

deedee: Well, *that* makes it perfectly clear.

trued: It's ridiculous, I know. But seeing him on
TV, where we watch all those fake shows
every day with actors and sets and make-
up . . . It suddenly hit me that he's *not*
acting, he's not playing a part that he can
leave at the end of the day.

deedee: Of course not.

trued: I'M TRYING TO FIGURE THIS OUT.

deedee: Okay. You don't have to scream.

trued: I'm sorry. It's actually nice of you to listen. I mean, you're not really *listening*, it's more like reading your screen. But I appreciate it.

deedee: Not a problem.

trued: But why did I think I could cure him? Why did I want to change him?

deedee: You tell me.

trued: Maybe I'm afraid.

deedee: Of?

trued: Of . . . of moving on without him. Maybe I'm worried about growing up and leaving him behind. That if I cured him, it would be safe for both of us to grow up.

deedee: I'm not a psychologist, but maybe all along *you've* been the one afraid to grow up.

trued: No. Absolutely not.

deedee: Then you're the only person I know who isn't.

trued: Really?

deedee: Sure, everybody fears the unknown. It would be nice if life were a bowl of cherries all the time, but that's not the way it is.

trued: A bowl of cherries? You sound like my mother!

deedee: SORRY!

trued: That's okay. But . . . but what about Eddie?

deedee: Why don't you keep doing what you've been doing—minus looking for a cure, of course. Just being his sister and friend might be enough.

trued: Do you think so?

deedee: I'd bet on it.

trued: Do you have kids?

deedee: Two.

trued: They're really lucky.

deedee: THANK YOU!

trued: YOU'RE WELCOME!

We sign off after tying up the line for twenty minutes. I hope Mom doesn't notice the extra computer time on her monthly bill. But I feel better than I have in days. I run through the house looking for Eddie, and I finally find him across the street at Jerry's. I grab the Frisbee from his hand and toss it into the air. It sails forward through the morning sky and lands squarely on the roof of Jerry's garage. Up, up, and away. Well, kind of.

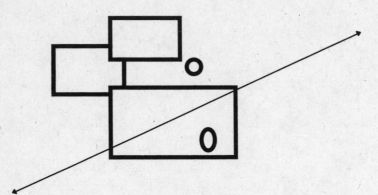

Moving on, alone and together
—Eddie Walker

A Slight Misunderstanding

At my meeting with Ms. Morelli at the cable station, I review my ideas for the upcoming season. More *Real Life* with Eddie, plus a variety show called (you'll never guess) *The Trudy Walker Show*. She interrupts me halfway through.

"We were looking to fill a half-hour slot with local programming," she says, peering over her glasses. "Not give someone a weekly show of their own."

I interrupt her right back. "But the response was so good, I thought you'd be interested in a few more shows."

"If we had any open slots, we'd definitely consider you," she says. "The audience feedback was very enthusiastic."

"But the newspaper said . . . "

"I'm sorry you misunderstood the article. Or maybe it was just wishful thinking."

My cheeks flush with embarrassment. I fish around my backpack for the file with all the letters from the cable company. "You never said anything about just one show."

"Trudy, here's what I wanted to talk to you about. Maybe it'll be something that interests you." She pulls her chair over to mine. "We're scheduling a teen variety show for the holidays. Kids from all over the city will participate."

"You want to know if I'll tape it?" Some consolation prize to having my own weekly show.

"Actually we were wondering if you'd host it."

"Really?" Images of lights, snow machines, and chorus lines fill my mind. "How about calling it *The Trudy Walker Show*? Might be kind of catchy. Eddie can have his own segment and my friend Denise can be my sidekick."

"Let's not get too ahead of ourselves," she says. "Right now we're just talking about you."

I need to think about it for all of two seconds. "I'll do it."

I leave the office, clenching and unclenching my fists. Yes! Walking through the hall, I see a giant *Jaws* poster falling off the wall. I take it down and hand it to the receptionist on my way out. Right now, no more sharks for me.

The Mysterious Deedee

I am at the mall with Denise splitting a chocolate shake. I spent the entire afternoon trying to
drag her into the record and book stores, when all
she wanted to do was try on earrings, but we still
had fun. No one approached me and asked for an
autograph, but that was okay, too. (When I'm rich
and famous I will probably do anything to get my
privacy back.) We share our shake and take turns
doing impersonations of Mr. Manning. Denise's is
the funniest—when she leans back to laugh, tiny
bits of chocolate spit from her nose. The waitress
asks us ten times if we're ready to leave. I tell
her no.

We wait outside for my mother to pick us up,
pretending to hitchhike when a cute guy drives by.
A blue Toyota that looks like my mother's pulls
up, so I head toward it.

"That's not your mother's," Denise says. "The
license plate is wrong."

"I don't even know what her license plate is,"
I say.

"I don't even know what her license plate is," Denise repeats, just to annoy me. "Two-four-three DEE. I bet Eddie would know."

I stop in the middle of the parking lot and a woman in a pickup beeps at me. I move back to Denise on the sidewalk. "D-E-E? Are you sure?"

"Tru, if you weren't so busy trying to get to Hollywood, you'd notice the little details in life."

Dee . . . Naaah, it can't be her. When I had my conversation with **deedee** last Saturday, my mother was working. Of course, she *does* have a computer at work. And that computer is *probably* on the Net. And **deedee**'s e-mail address *did* seem like a company name. And **deedee** *did* say she had two kids. Could my mother have spotted the on-line messages addressed to her screen name and written me back with a different one? No way. She'd never be able to keep a secret like that.

When her car pulls up, Denise and I get in.

"Did you have fun?" she asks.

"Yes, DEEDEE," I say.

Denise looks at me like I've eaten some bad ice cream.

"Huh, Mom?" I say, leaning over the front seat, nudging her.

"Tru, I have no idea what you're talking about," my mother answers. She asks Denise how her family is doing.

"Do they have e-mail at the company you've been working at these past few months?" I interrupt.

"Everybody has e-mail nowadays," she says, and then continues talking to Denise.

I can feel myself getting mad—betrayed, deceived. Then, just as quickly, I decide I don't want to wreck such a fun day, so I roll down the window and let my anger fly outside. It's a visualization trick even my mother would be proud of.

"I'd love to go to the movies tonight," my mother suggests.

Denise and I run through what is playing at the local theater, but the whole time I am staring at the back of my mother's head. Her hair is still brown, but the gray is more noticeable, especially braided the way it is now. I lean right next to her face.

"The movies would be great," I say.

"The apples don't fall far from the trees," she answers.

I smile at the cliché—one of her more stupid ones—and realize it doesn't matter if she is **deedee** or not. Actually, maybe we've stumbled on a good setup—she can leave her opinions on the computer and I don't have to feel like I'm taking advice from my mother. Even without Eddie in the car, we sing the Kookaburra Song on the way home, and play Chinese Fire Drill in front of the high school. Denise is embarrassed that my mother is running around the car, too, but I just grab on to Mom's plaid jacket and run. I check out the license plate as I race by.

Nah.

What Are You Going to Do Now That You've Finished Your TV Show? I'm Going to Disney World! (Well, Not Really . . .)

We are all eating breakfast Thursday morning—bagels and cream cheese, except for Eddie who has bagels and ketchup—when my mother makes an announcement.

"You're not going to school today," she says.

I ask her what she's talking about.

"And I'm not going to work. We're all playing hooky until Monday."

Eddie runs to the back door and brings his hockey stick into the kitchen. "Hip check!"

"Not hockey," I tell him. *"Hooky."*

Mom takes the hockey stick from Eddie and pretends to hit a slap shot. "We're taking a little trip," she says.

I cross my fingers under my seat and hope. Could what I'm thinking possibly be true?

"We're getting dressed," she continues, "getting in the car, and going to . . . Super World."

"Where?!"

"Well, I know you two have been wanting to go to Disney World for years, but we just can't afford it right now. I thought this might be fun."

I uncross my fingers and push my bagel away. The story of my life—one big consolation prize. She holds her arms out, sensing my disappointment. "Tru, it's the best I can do, okay?"

What can you say when someone lets you down while trying their best to make you happy? I've never even *heard* of Super World, which is probably in some family's backyard, with toys instead of rides. Still we *are* talking about missing two days of school . . . Eddie and I go upstairs to pack.

We drive for five hours, singing and playing license plate games on the way. (Eddie keeps yelling "I found one!" even when he doesn't know what we're looking for.) At the motel, there are two double beds in one room. My mother and I take one and Eddie takes the other. When my mother goes down the hall to get ice, Eddie and I put on the little shower caps from the bathroom and jump up and down on the beds. My mother comes back in the room, takes one look at us, climbs on the bed, and starts jumping, too.

The next morning we eat pancakes for breakfast and follow the map to Super World. I try not to let my disappointment show when we pull into the

parking lot. Weeds have grown through the pave-
ment, which is littered with empty cups and bags.
The Super World sign is chipped and the letter *p* is
missing.

"Sewer World," I say. "Here we are."

My mother makes a face to shut me up. We lock
up the car and buy tickets.

Inside the gate, the rides are dull and worn, even
the man selling balloons looks like he doesn't want
to be there. So much for the Magic Kingdom.

That is, until I see Eddie.

Eddie runs to the merry-go-round as if the
horses are alive, jumping up and down in line,
waiting for the music to end and his turn to come.
When it stops, my mother hands him a ticket and
he races to a large blue stallion, yelling "Giddyap!"
as he climbs on. One of the horse's ears is broken,
and the blue is so faded it's almost gray, but Eddie
holds on to the reigns as if he's galloping along the
prairie. I join my mother, who attempts a smile.

"It's almost Disney World for him," she says.
"Sorry it's not the same for you."

"It's okay," I answer. "Some of the rides look
fun." And when I finally can pry Eddie off the
horse—five rides later—we head for the roller
coaster.

We try different rides all morning, then eat tacos
under a tree for lunch. On the bumper cars, Eddie

and I crash into several people, while Eddie makes loud police siren noises. The man at the controls tells us to be quiet, but I point to Eddie and say he can't help it. (My mother hates it when I use Eddie's handicap as an excuse to misbehave.)

My mother asks the park manager to stay with Eddie for a few minutes while she and I go on some rides together. Because we have to do so many special things for Eddie, she always tries to make sure we do things just for me sometimes. We go on the Water Slide, the Turbo Car, and Moonbeam Mountain. She screams a little bit on the first bump, then the two of us start screaming the whole time, like little kids. When we meet the manager and Eddie near the souvenir shop, Eddie is telling her that he's on television. I'm sure she's thinking, Yeah, right. Sure you are.

At the end of the day, Eddie won't leave without going on the ducky ride. It's a kiddie ride, with these stupid duck cars that slowly spin round and round in circles. Even a few hundred miles from home, I won't be caught dead on it, so Eddie goes on it alone.

The park is closing and my mother and I sit on the bench near the ticket booth watching Eddie go around, waving each time he passes us. My mother looks at me and smiles kind of sadly. I know what she is thinking: that even though we are twins, I will outgrow the kiddie rides and the cartoon characters, but not Eddie. I think ahead, of Eddie and I older—maybe twenty or twenty-five—and picture him grown up, maybe even in a suit, still on this ride, waving and smiling in place, with the sunset bright behind him.

When the ride stops, I run to the woman at the controls and hand her two tickets. Eddie is so excited that I have decided to come on the ride with him that he jumps up and down in the seat. I squeeze next to him inside the duck and we ride round and round, waving to my mother on each turn. For now, I'm happy just to be in his orbit, spinning into our separate futures, however long the journey takes.

Well?
What are you waiting for?
Do you think I'm going to sit here forever and
spill my guts for your entertainment pleasure?

Log off!

Just kidding . . .

But maybe not . . .

As we say in television:

THE END

Epilogue

Trudy Walker is now a famous filmmaker living with her family in a lavish town house in Boston's Back Bay. Her projects include a three-picture deal with A-list movie stars and a medical documentary entitled *Eddie*. Her computer journal, *Tru Confessions*, was called "the most innovative piece of journalism this year" by Columbia University. She, her friend Denise, and her brother, Eddie, frequently travel to Europe on her private jet, which is stocked with vintage films, candied apples, and ice cream. Her cable show has won three Ace Awards for best local programming, and Eddie's recent exhibit at the Museum of Modern Art in New York, *Technical Difficulties*, was hailed as the most important cultural event of the season.

(It will all be tru, just wait. Hey, what are dreams for if you don't believe in them. . . .)

GO FISH

JANET TASHJIAN

What did you want to be when you grew up?
Students ask me this all the time and I wish I had a better answer. When I was young, I was too busy playing, reading, and studying to think about career goals. I envy people who knew what they wanted to be by age ten. I was not one of them.

When did you realize you wanted to be a writer?
My husband and I traveled around the world together, and when we got back to the States, we had to fill in several forms. One asked for 'occupation' and I put down 'writer' even though I'd never done anything more than dabble. But deep down, I always felt being a writer would be the greatest job in the world. It took me several years after that to make that dream a reality.

What's your first childhood memory?
I remember cooking candies in a little pan on a toy stove I got for Christmas. I was maybe three. I'm not

sure if I remember it or if I just saw the photograph so often that I think I do.

What's your most embarrassing childhood memory?
I was singing and dancing in a school assembly with my first-grade class when my shoe fell off. I kept going without the shoe, hopping around the stage—the show must go on.

What was your worst subject in school?
I always did well in school, but for some reason I forgot all my math skills and now can barely multiply. I'd love to know where all my math skills went.

What was your first job?
I've had dozens of jobs since I was sixteen—working on assembly lines, tutoring, babysitting, washing dishes, waiting tables, delivering dental molds and telephone books, selling copy machines, working in a fabric store, painting houses—I could fill a whole page with how many jobs I've had.

How did you celebrate publishing your first book?
By inviting my tenth-grade English teacher to my first book signing. The photo of the two of us from that day sits on my writing desk.

Where do you write your books?
Usually in my office in the house. But because I often write in longhand, I end up writing everywhere—on the beach, in a coffee shop, wherever I am.

Where do you find inspiration for your writing?
Everywhere—there's nothing more interesting or wacky than real life. A word in a book, a bit of conversation in an elevator, something I find in the street. I find dozens of ideas a day. Real life is amazing.

Which of your characters is most like you?
They all have pieces of me. I love words like Marty Frye; I can be a bit obsessive like Monica in *Multiple Choice;* I have the same ambition and persistence as Trudy in *Tru Confessions;* the same striving for the funny as Becky in *Fault Line.* Larry [also from *Fault Line*] is also very much like me—getting carried away with new ideas while trying to stay focused. We're both big believers in average people trying to change the world.

When you finish a book, who reads it first?
Usually my editor, Christy. Sometimes my husband, Doug. Her [Christy's] feedback is much more helpful; he [Doug] always thinks what I write is great.

How do you usually feel once you've completed a manuscript? Are you ever sad when a book you are writing is over?
Relieved! I don't really miss my characters; they're always with me.

Are you a morning person or a night owl?
I like waking up early and getting right to work. I'm too fried by the end of the day to get anything substantial done.

What's your idea of the best meal ever?
Something healthy and fresh with lots of friends sitting around talking. Definitely a chocolate dessert.

Which do you like better: cats or dogs?
I love dogs and always have one. I'm allergic to cats so I stay away from them. They don't seem as much fun as dogs anyway.

What do you value most in your friends?
A sense of humor and dependability. All my friends are pretty funny.

Where do you go for peace and quiet?
Like Larry [from *Fault Line*], I head for the woods. I'm there all the time. I love the beach, too.

What makes you laugh out loud?
My son. He's by far the funniest person I know.

What's your favorite song?
Anything by Todd Rundgren, Joni Mitchell, Richard Thompson, or Elvis Costello. Geniuses, all of them. I also love U2's "Bad." I always have a list of songs in mind for every book I write. I wish each book could come with a CD. Music is a very important part of the writing process for me.

Who is your favorite fictional character?
As if I could choose just one!

What are you most afraid of?

I worry about all the normal mom things like war, drunk drivers, and strange illnesses with no cures. I'm also afraid our culture is veering away from basic things like nature. I worry about the implications down the road.

What time of the year do you like best?

The summer, absolutely. I hate the cold.

What is your favorite TV show?

I mostly watch British television. Their comedies are outrageous and their dramas are riveting. I also like anything with Ricky Gervais.

If you were stranded on a desert island, who would you want for company?

My family!

If you could travel in time, where would you go?

To the future, to see how badly we've messed things up.

What's the best advice you have ever received about writing?

To do it as a daily practice, like running or meditation.

How do you react when you receive criticism?

My sales background and MFA workshops left me with a very tough skin. If the feedback makes the book better, bring it on.

What do you want readers to remember about your books?
I want them to remember the characters as if they were old friends.

What would you do if you ever stopped writing?
Try to live my life without finding stories everywhere. For a job, I'd be doing some kind of design—anything from renovating houses to creating fabric.

What do you like best about yourself?
I am not afraid of work.

What is your worst habit?
I hate to exercise.

What do you consider to be your greatest accomplishment?
How great my son is.

What do you wish you could do better?
Write a perfect first draft.

What would your readers be most surprised to learn about you?
I litter McDonald's trash out my car window while I drive—KIDDING!

What is your favorite noise or sound?
My son laughing really hard.

Did you keep a journal like Trudy when you were growing up? Do you write in one now?
I'm so busy writing books, the last thing I want to do in my spare time is write in a journal.

What is your idea of fun?
Walking through New York City at night.

Is there anything you'd like to confess?
I love dark chocolate.

What would your friends say if we asked them about you?
She acts like a fifteen-year-old boy.

What's on your list of things to do right now?
Update my Web site.

What are some things you think about when you're bored?
Story ideas.

How do you spend a rainy day?
Watching comedy DVDs with my son.

Can you share a little-known fact about yourself?
I love to make collages.

SQUARE FISH